D1478250

Veronica

# WARRIOR
## OF TRUTH

Enjoy and please remain true to
yourself and others. When you
are, you are following your correct
path here on Mother Earth.
    Thank You
        Ev        7/12/10

# WARRIOR OF TRUTH

The True Meaning and Purpose
on Mother Earth Revealed

## EV MURRAY

Tate Publishing & Enterprises

*Warrior of Truth: The True Meaning and Purpose on Mother Earth Revealed*
Copyright © 2007 by Ev Murray. All rights reserved.

This title is also available as a Tate Out Loud product. Visit www.tatepublishing.com for more information.

No part of this publication may be reproduced, stored in a retrieval system or transmitted in any way by any means, electronic, mechanical, photocopy, recording or otherwise without the prior permission of the author except as provided by USA copyright law.

The opinions expressed by the author are not necessarily those of Tate Publishing, LLC.

Published by Tate Publishing & Enterprises, LLC
127 E. Trade Center Terrace | Mustang, Oklahoma 73064 USA
1.888.361.9473 | www.tatepublishing.com

Tate Publishing is committed to excellence in the publishing industry. The company reflects the philosophy established by the founders, based on Psalms 68:11,
*"The Lord gave the word and great was the company of those who published it."*

Book design copyright © 2007 by Tate Publishing, LLC. All rights reserved.
*Cover design and Interior design by Jacob Crissup*

Published in the United States of America
ISBN: 978-1-60247-731-5
1. Fiction    2. Native American
07.10.01

# INTRODUCTION

This story is narrated by the Warrior of Truth. Before he walked Mother Earth, while he walked Mother Earth, and after he left Mother Earth. The stories true purpose has a special meaning for all who read it. Hopefully it's understood and felt; Love for life, here and now, at our present time on Mother Earth.

# FOREWORD

Ev lived with The Warrior of Truth a very long time. The story came to him in bits and pieces, over many years, and it never went away. It is a story that wanted to be told, and it wanted to be told by Ev.

As a child, Ev was always outdoors, roaming the woods, and climbing the mountains. He was always one with the energy of the Mother, the Earth. He thought everyone grew up feeling that connection and knowing how to tap into it. He thought everyone knew how to stop and listen and feel and breathe in—how to be quiet enough, to sense your own direction, to hear the truth inside yourself, to know what is real, to be your own compass. To be your own compass is something we all have to be—no one else can know the right direction for another—we each have to follow our own truth.

Of Iroquois descent, Ev spent a lot of time with his maternal grandparents. He learned how to live with the land, how to hunt with bow and arrow, respecting all forms of life, taking only what would be used "so the People may live." Ev loved to listen to his grandparent's stories. His grandfather taught him how to work with his hands. "The Warrior of Truth" began to come through to Ev in those early quiet moments, the story revealing itself in its own time. Woodworking and handcrafts are still a very important part of Ev's life. Everything he does has a meaning.

Ev began to write the story down when he was sixteen. At that time he was in high school helping one of his teachers lead canoe trips to the North Country lakes. After high school, Ev volunteered to go into the Air Force during the Viet Nam War. The purpose he felt inside himself was to help others survive. His assignment was working with survival equipment in Tan Son Nhut Air Base, Saigon. His approach was not adversarial, "here you are, learn how to survive against all odds…" His approach was to teach each person how to touch his or her inner knowing—how to "keep their head on straight" while in life—threatening situations. The common thread was to show each person how to survive by finding his or her own truth—how to find that place within yourself where the right direction makes itself known, no matter what may surround you at any given time. The space that allows you to be in your "truth" and all else falls away, and you know what needs to be done.

As the years went by, Ev began to understand that the story of Buffalo Tear, White Cloud, Peace, and the others—the story that was always with him—was actually a way to share this knowing of "truth" with others. He needed to find a way to let the story be told to a larger audience.

Ev bought a computer and learned how to use it. Nights and early mornings, he wrote down the story that had lived inside of him for so many years. He found what notes he could and remembered the rest and new parts of the story came through. When his computer crashed and all his work was lost, he never even considered giving up—he simply bought another computer and began again. He had no idea what he would do with the story once it was on paper, he just knew he had to get it into a readable form.

That is when I first met Ev. He was closing his computer one day and came across my name while he was looking for a publisher. It just popped up. Neither one of us believes in accidents. This was a new beginning. Ev called my number and spoke with my son, who thought we were certainly meant to meet. I had been a Pipe carrier for many years, studied and practiced the Native American ways. It took some time, but we finally got together, and I read Ev's story. I could feel the purpose in Ev and in "The Warrior of Truth," and I became one of his strongest supporters to get this story out to others.

There is Native American understanding about what is alive, what is a part of divine energy, what is real. "If it casts a shadow, it has Spirit." Everything is a part of Great Spirit, and Spirit is a part of everything—no exceptions, nothing separate, nothing could be—we are all one. In the moments when we feel that understanding, we are in touch with "truth"—we know we are part of each other, an what we do to others we do to ourselves—we are all made from the Mother, made of this Earth, and we are, in that way, all one. At any moment of time, in any situation, we can breathe in, align with this understanding, know our own direction, and know what we need to do. And then, there is choice.

There is a peace that you can feel in the presence of one who knows his or her own truth. It is a peace that is strong, like the center of gravity, powerful and simply there with no question. It is an alignment of the heart, mind, spirit and energy that is us—beyond us and part of us at the same time—Great Spirit—a part of everything that casts a shadow. And there is no question it is real. "Heart alignment" is what I have always felt in Ev. I feel it in the "Warrior of Truth," and I know it is real.

So, dear readers, take this journey with Ev to the Sacred Mountain. You don't have to believe anything, just go with him on this journey and enjoy—and blessings on your way.

—Penelope Jewell
2/2/07
Author of "A Master's Path" and "A Guide to Your Practice of Reiki Energy Healing"

## PREFACE

With each step taken on your way to the mountaintop something is learned. Listen: you will hear. Look: you will see. Touch: you will feel. Search: you will find. Live: you will learn. Open minds and hearts. Brings truth, wisdom, and knowledge. Follow your path with strength and courage. We are all a part of each other, respect and honor and you will be. All of life is connected and when one becomes extinct so does a part of us. In all beginnings there is an ending, in all endings there is a new beginning, like a circle. The cycle now is only a speck on the circle and it continues until it all becomes one. When you are looking for answers the answer is always there. It's not what you bring with you to find it but what you leave with that matters and makes the difference. When it is time to leave the present, what one has touched and said will always remain in plain view for those left behind with open hearts and souls. Beauty of love is always there, seek it out and it will be seen, felt, heard, and smelled. Some steps could be difficult to take to the top of the mountain, but you must always continue.

Because the closer you get, the brighter the light becomes and the stronger you become. At the top you will have all that you have ever wished and dreamed for.

**PART 1**

# CHAPTER ONE

It was early morning on a spring day. The sky was a beautiful blue with long narrow white clouds, and a steady light breeze. A sound in the distance had gathered Buffalo Tear's people to the stream at the westward side of their village. They knew the different sounds of Mother Nature's wild side, but this crying was not the sound of a Mountain Lion. A baby Mountain Lion at times will sound like a human baby crying.

The warriors of the tribe were ready to leave and search for whom or what was making the wild sound. Buffalo Tear stood in silence facing the sun in a deep meditative state. He was not only the chief, but also a medicine man for his people. Buffalo Tear was taller than any of his people and he had seen over twenty-five years of life on Mother Earth. His hair was long and black with some silver streaks running through his braids. The silver streaks in his hair had been there sinse his birth. They represented the symbol of goodness within him for his people.

The warriors had already worked out their plan of attack,

assuming that the sound could be a threat or enemy to their people and village. Red Feather, the most honored warrior in the village, gathered up his fellow warriors and started out across the stream. As they reached the outer bank, Buffalo Tear came out of his meditative state.

The warriors slipped into the dense forest at the foot of the huge mountain, which was a sacred place to the Indian village of Buffalo Tear. Because of its size, the natives felt that the mountain helped the ones who left Mother Earth enter the heavens by following the path to the top. For Buffalo Tear, the mountain was also his place of visions. He would often spend several days in meditation at the mountaintop to help his people in their every day life events.

When Buffalo Tear turned to his people to speak, he then realized that the warriors had left. Running Deer was standing next to him, holding her newborn baby girl, Morning Mist, in her arms close to her heart.

Buffalo Tear spoke, "I have seen what is to be and all I can say for now is that I must go and stop the warriors. For a great gift has been given to us, for our survival until the end of time."

Running Deer pointed out the direction in which the warriors had gone. The sound of crying suddenly stopped, but Buffalo Tear knowing every inch of ground of the mountain, had a good idea where to start his search. As he crossed the stream, he looked back to his people and waved, for he loved them all. He entered the forest and began to think back in time when he was a very young man.

Buffalo Tear's first adventure to the base of the mountain was a test of his manhood, the same test that all the young Indian men would have to pass to prove their ability not only to themselves, but to their people as well. After two weeks in the snowy forest, Buffalo Tear returned to his village only to find that an enemy tribe had attacked them. Many of his people were wounded and most of the village food supply was taken. He and only a few young warriors had to save the village people from starvation. They hunted for days, but they were unable to bring enough food back to their village for their people. The wounded warriors were dying yet they would give their portion of food to the old, women, and children.

A warrior named Hawk called Buffalo Tear over to his side. Hawk looked deeply into Buffalo Tear's eyes, gripped his hand and said. "Take this feather and go to the very top of the mountain and ask our ancestors for help. You must first cleanse your body and soul in the smoke hut before you go. When you are given a sign, go to the mountaintop with an open heart and soul." The warrior took a deep breath and with great effort said, "Be strong young one." Those were his last words.

All warriors would go to the smoke hut to prepare themselves before a hunt or battle. Cleansing oneself spiritually and physically and entering a deep meditative state of mind, would sometimes take a few days before they would feel ready for the task at hand.

The smoke hut was dark and the air was heavy with the smell of cedar wood and sage. It was very difficult to breathe inside the smoke hut. In the darkness, the feather that Hawk had given Buffalo Tear began to glow. Holding it straight out from his body, the feather became so brilliant that the smoke hut was filled with a white light. This was the sign for Buffalo Tear to go to the mountaintop. The climb was very difficult, not only because of the winter snow, but also because of the lack of food for strength in his body. Finally at the mountaintop, the feather began to glow bright again. Looking through the feather at a distance, which looked like miles away, there were dark figures moving. These figures were buffalo and they were heading toward the village. With strength from within, young Buffalo Tear raced down the mountain and told the other young ones what had happened. None of the young Indians had ever hunted the Buffalo before, but they knew the hunt could be the only chance for their people's survival.

The herd of buffalo was moving slowly across the snow-covered plains. The young warriors were not sure how they were even going to get close enough to get a shot off with their bows an arrows without spooking the herd. They split up and formed a semicircle on a small knoll in front of the herd. Lying in the cold snow waiting for the buffalo to get within range was another test of will and strength for them.

It was time and with a battle scream they all stood and shot their arrows. The buffalo herd separated and ran in different directions. One large buffalo came running full bore, straight at Buffalo Tear. But the buffalo suddenly stopped only a couple of feet away, staring at the white feather that hung from the top of Buffalo Tear's bow. The buffalo then did something no Indian had ever seen before; he put his large horned head down, and laid his body down in the snow. Buffalo Tear released the arrow from his bow and it entered the Buffalo's heart. The young warriors could not believe what they had just witnessed. They all came running over only to see a young warrior with tears on his cheek kneeling at the side of the buffalo.

Buffalo Tear spoke, "This buffalo has given us his life, and we must always honor and respect him for doing this." The young warriors all shook their heads in agreement.

One spoke up and said, "Yes, we shall and your name from this day forward will be known as 'Buffalo Tear' in his honor."

Buffalo Tear, reached down to his right side and touched the buffalo horn and white feather, the same ones that had been with him all his days. Through all the years, these two items had helped him and his people in times of great need. Buffalo Tear knew that the feather and the horn would lead his way to what he had seen in his vision by the stream this day.

He then began to pick up his pace, but he stopped because he heard two new sounds; a wolf was howling loudly, and an eagle screaming while in flight. Suddenly there was the sound of something running up on his right side, Buffalo Tear stood completely motionless as the running came nearer. Then, there it was, running full force, straight toward him. The white wolf only blinked its eyes as it ran by so swift that it was like its feet weren't even touching the ground. Buffalo Tear had seen many wolves in his life, but never one so beautiful. He knew that this wolf was very different then the others; he could sense the power and strength of this very special animal. Buffalo Tear stepped over to follow the wolf's trail because he felt that it was going to lead him to his vision. Looking down to where the tracks should have been, Buffalo Tear saw that there were no tracks to be found. He knew that it was a sign for him to hurry up.

Buffalo Tear then broke out into a full sprint up the hill. After about a half mile of running he heard the eagle scream loudly again ahead and to his left. Buffalo Tear's legs and lungs were in pain so he began to slow down his pace. Looking up he noticed a clearing in the tree line. He knew the exact location and headed straight for it. He stopped a few feet into the clearing. Above him and straight up the mountain a bird in circling flight took his breath away. Again, he had never seen anything like it before. In his life he had witnessed many wonders, but this was truly the first of its kind. This bird was not anything ordinary; it was the biggest and most beautiful Eagle he had ever seen. Like the white wolf, this eagle was pure white as well.

Buffalo Tear broke out into an all-out run again in the direction of the circling white eagle. He knew that his vision was about to become reality, even though he wasn't exactly sure what it was he was going to discover. But he did know that his people and all others were going to have a very special journey ahead of them. All of a sudden, an arrow flew across his chest, leaving only a small cut. Looking in the direction from which the arrow came he could see one of his village warriors lying still with blood soaked earth around him. What he didn't see was another warrior in a tree with his bow an arrow at full draw, pointed at his heart. Suddenly there was a white streak from the sky that hit the warrior in the tree so hard that when his body hit the ground his head was missing. Buffalo Tear could see the streak slowing down and as it did it materialized into the white eagle.

Buffalo Tear walked over to check out his villager's body for any signs of life. When he touched the warrior with his hand Buffalo Tear had a vision. Bear Claw had a courageous fight against five enemy warriors. Bear Claw was killed, but he had wounded all five of the warriors before he lost his life. As Buffalo Tear went to check out the enemy warrior's body, there was another warrior's battle cry, just a few hundred yards away. Looking at the enemy, he couldn't tell which tribe he was from, but on the center of his back was a black mark shaped like a circle. All warriors painted themselves to show their strength and maybe to also frighten their foe.

Buffalo Tear could hear the running of feet in the direction of the battle cry. All of his senses needed to be in their highest atonement in order to accomplish this mission of wonderment.

Red Feather, Spotted Rabbit, and Running Elk were the only warriors left in the group of Indian warriors from Buffalo Tear's village. While they were moving their way up the mountain to the sound of the wild cries, they were ambushed. They fought bravely, but they were out numbered and this surprise attack put them at a great disadvantage. The three warriors that were still alive had to use not only their knowledge, but also their physical strength in order to survive this encounter with the enemy.

Buffalo Tear all of a sudden felt like "something" was trying to make him go away from the sound of running feet. This something was a familiar feeling, an energy he had felt before. He knew he needed to follow its direction. After a short distance he discovered small drops of blood on the ground. He followed this sign. He knew that if the blood trail continued in this direction that it would lead him to a place on the mountain that he called the Opening Gateway.

There were many special places on the mountain, but this one was the most beautiful. The tree line would end and the ground would be all wild flowers in the spring and summer. The view was three hundred sixty degrees. It was as if you were at the top of the world. And if you were to reach up above your head with your hands outstretched, you could touch the clouds in the sky that encircled the mountain.

Walking through the tall grass and wild flowers Buffalo Tear could see at the very crest of the mountain that someone was sitting with their back to him. As he got closer he could see that the individual was hurt and that it was a woman. When he came to her side she looked into his eyes and said, "I've been waiting for you. Please sit down for my time here is short." Buffalo Tear could see that she was correct because her dress was completely blood stained, and that at some point in time she had been tortured, because of the scars on her face, arms and legs.

"I have much to say and I also know that you will have many questions. But we have very little time and when it's over you must leave me here alone."

White Cloud touched Buffalo Tear's hand and asked him, "Please always guide and protect my son here on Mother Earth."

Buffalo Tear said, "You need not worry because I know what my duty is to be. But my question is, where is he?"

White Cloud smiled with tears in her eyes and said, "My son is in the oak cave and his friends are guarding him."

"I know the place and I also know his guardians," Buffalo Tear reached out and touched White Cloud's other hand. Together they sat with no other words spoken, because they were now as one.

In his mind's eye he could see that White Clouds life journey had been one full of many challenges. She was born in a village of peace and love for all things, but one day they were attacked and their home was no more. She was only a newborn at the time. Her people were tortured and than killed because they would not conform to the ways of their enemy. They would not give up their beliefs of love and goodness. This enemy tribe wanted all power and control over all life. If it meant destruction of their own people or anything living, it did not matter to them. They felt that nothing was going to stop them from total control over all life in this world.

As she became older, White Cloud was treated as an outcast by Dark Eye and his followers. She disagreed with their ways of doing things. The Tribal Counsel decided that it was time to remove her to the outskirts of the village. There an old woman lived who the village people consider a witch. She could heal the wounded warriors and sick from the village. Her use of herbal medicines and spells frightened the village people. Even the ones that were healed were afraid of her. They felt that instead of dying she brought them back to life. They were all very afraid of her powers.

The warriors of the tribe escorted White Cloud to the witch's mud and grass hut and told her that she was not allowed to enter the village without permission first. White Cloud was afraid of the witch in the beginning, but in time she came to see that she was a good person. She became her teacher in many ways, and White Cloud came to know her true self first. She learned how to help heal the sick and wounded people as well as the wild animals.

One evening the old one woke up White Cloud and said to her, "You come from wonderful people and you will return to them, but you must first fulfill your destiny. The path will be a painful one, but you are strong and must always depend on that strength to carry you through all that is to be. You have a very special purpose here so always follow and keep to your true self. It is my time, and I must now go to my ancestors.

You stay here for now, but follow your heart." White Cloud stood up and gave the old one a loving hug before she went out into the darkness of the night.

When the leaders of the village heard that the witch was no more, they held a meeting with White Cloud. They told her that she would be the new healer and that she was to remain at the hut under the same rules. She was to stay away from the people of the village and that they would bring the sick and wounded to her in exchange for food and water.

After a few months she began thinking about trying to escape, but she knew it would be difficult because she was being watched. She had seen them but she pretended that she hadn't, giving them a false reassurance in their spying ability.

It was a rainy day and when the evening came White Cloud felt the time was right for escape. She broke a hole into the back wall of the hut and crawled her way out and into the woods for a ways before she could stand up. Because of the rain and clouds, the forest was very dark; she had to move slowly and with caution because of the many dangers. After traveling all night, the morning sun was beginning to rise. Ahead she could hear the sound of water running swiftly. The river was very wide and would have been too difficult to swim in. Walking along the riverbank she spotted a large piece of driftwood. She waded into the water and pushed it out into the swift current. She held on tight as she floated down through the rapids on it. The water was very cold which was good because every once and awhile her body, legs, and arms would hit rocks. What she didn't realize was that some of the hits were on sharp rocks which left deep cuts on her body. With the water being so cold it helped the pain and bleeding not to be felt. But after awhile she began to feel light headed and weak. She decided it was time to try and work her way back to the riverbank. She was only a few yards away when the speed of the current picked up greatly. The next feeling was one of falling and she was because she had just gone over a fifty-foot waterfall.

Buffalo Tear held White Clouds hand gently and asked her, "Are we about to meet the father of our people's new teacher?"

White Cloud said, "Yes, and Buffalo Tear. At the end of this, if I am no longer here, please take my body over to that ledge. You will know what to do next, my brother."

"Yes, I will, my sister."

White Cloud opened up her eyes and the light was so bright it was hard to make out the human form standing above her. His words were so soft and full of love, "You will be okay. Don't be afraid. You are safe and you will be healed soon. The river has scarred and broken your body very badly, but you are a special woman; pure of heart and soul." White Cloud's eyes and mind began to take focus on the man and the surroundings. She was lying on a bed of flowers that made her feel as if she were floating on air. The sky was a deep beautiful blue with the sun shining very bright. There was also a light wind blowing that brought the smell of all of Mother Earth's beauty. The man standing who was in focus now was also a wonder of beauty. "Who are you?"

"This may be a little hard to understand, White Cloud. But if you keep your heart and mind open to me, you will know all, and from this day forward you will be at my side. You still have some unfinished work, but at the end we will be as one. My name was given to me by my parents, Mother Earth and Father Sun. And their names were given to them by the Creator of all things in our world. I have been sent here for a very special purpose. Our people are losing their way. Material things, greed, power and control, different beliefs, not being equal and respectful is destroying all that is living. I can only remain in this physical form for a short time. You know that I have been chosen and you have been chosen to give the human race a new teacher. And only if you are willing can this be. I have followed you though your journey this far and will continue to be with you always. After you have accomplished this part of your life, we will be together as one to help guide and protect our son through his journey. I'm called the Warrior of Peace; our son's words will be ones of truth and guidance to our people. And one day he to will walk with and be a guardian to all life."

White Cloud looked deep into Peace's eyes and said, "Thank you, I am honored to have been chosen." She could feel the strength of love that was felt for her from Peace.

"I am honored to, and so are our ancestors, to have such a giving soul as yours." He then touched his lips to her lips and their love flowed through them both.

White Cloud opened her eyes. She was on a sandy shore of the river. The sun was going down on the West Bank as she sat up. She looked at her arms and legs. They were healed, but there were many scars from the wounds she had received. She understood what had just happened, while touching the ground and looking toward the sun she spoke.

"Thank you, my Creator. I am your servant. Please help

keep me strong and I will fulfill your wishes. I will follow the correct path and fear no evil."

As she stood up, there was a noise in the woods. The large grizzly bear that had been watching her was hungry and he was about to attack. But as he approached, his feeling for food changed to a feeling of protection. He walked over to her slowly and stood at her side. White Cloud touched the top of his head with her hand and spoke to him softly. "When I first saw you, I was frightened, but Peace told me that you were here to protect me, so I thank you for your help, my friend."

After a few days, the grizzly bear and White Cloud became close and the main reason for this was the respect they felt for each other.

Back at the village from which she had escaped, the high council was very mad because no one had escaped from them before, especially a woman. So they had sent out many groups of warriors to catch her and bring her back to make an example of her. The warriors were told that they would be highly rewarded for this task.

After a couple months of searching most of the warriors returned to the village, they were told to go back out to the northwest and follow the river to the waterfalls. There you will follow the trail of a group of other warriors that discovered signs of White Cloud's trail. They also noticed the grizzly tracks, but figured that the bear was after her as well.

It had been a long period of time since White Cloud had seen another human, but she was very healthy and happy because of the new life she felt moving in her body. With each passing day, she could feel the child's strength growing and that his time would be soon. White Cloud was looking forward to holding her son and sharing him with the world. Peace would come to White Cloud whenever she asked to be with him. He would always come with great love for her and his son and speak of things that were going to happen, so that she would understand the end and the new beginning. She was not afraid of the end because she knew of all the good it would bring to those in need of hope and a new understanding of the life that had been forgotten.

White Cloud was about to leave the forest and go out into a wide-open grassy plain area. In the distance she saw the birthplace of her son, a large mountain. After she moved a few steps out in the grass a warrior appeared and approached her.

Then more warriors came from the forest behind her and one said, "White Cloud, you are to come with us back to our village, and who is the father of that child whom you carry inside you? Gray Rabbit, go back to Dark Eye and tell him we found White Cloud. "

"You will not understand, but I will tell you this. My child is to be a special gift, for I have been blessed by our Creator."

"Stop it, you witch! I think I will leave this child right here," he pulled out his knife and ran straight at White Cloud. As he was about to slash open her belly, a large roar came from the tree line behind the warriors. Before they could turn around the bear attacked, two warriors were down before they could respond to his force.

As he jumped to the third warrior, three arrows were shot into him. The bear didn't slow down his speed; he turned and attacked the archers. Before he had reached them, three more arrows entered his body. He was hurt badly and knew that his time was soon to be over. Six warriors were down. The only one left was holding a knife on White Cloud's belly. As the bear walked slowly toward them, White Cloud's eyes filled with tears for her friend and protector. The bear stopped and fell to the ground at the warrior's feet.

The warrior then turned to White Cloud and said, "You witch! You have killed my warriors and now I will do the same to you." As he brought his knife arm up to strike her in the heart, two huge bear legs reached up and grabbed him, then pulled him down to his body. The knife did cut White Cloud, but it wasn't a critical wound. The warrior turned on the bear's body and he began to stab the bear. The bear reached up with his hind legs and gripped onto the warrior's lower body, and with a last effort he pulled the warriors body in half.

White Cloud kneeled at the bear's side and touched his face and said. "I will walk at your side again, my friend. Go to Peace. He will help guide you on your new journey. I thank you." She kissed his face, "Go with love, my guardian and friend." He pointed to the mountain with his leg and turned and looked at the mountain. Then he closed his eyes. She knew that he was telling her that it was time for her to go to the mountain.

It took three days for White Cloud to reach the base of the mountain. She began to make her way up the mountain, but she felt tired and weak. She knew she needed to rest to regain her physical strength because her body was totally exhausted. She felt that the birth of her son would be soon so she needed to find a place of safety. White Cloud sat down under a huge oak tree, her eyes closed and she fell to sleep. When she woke up she knew that she had to find the place quickly for the birth of her son. As she stood up, White Cloud noticed an opening in the side of the mountain. She got down on her hands and knees and went threw the opening.

Inside the entry there was a large cave and she found everything she would need for his birth. There was a spot that had many handmade blankets that would make a comfortable bed and there was also food and water. She knew that someone else used this place, but she felt safe here. This was where she was going to give her son life.

When the other group of warriors came to the battle area they became enraged with anger. They decided that White Cloud would die a slow and painful death when she was captured. They headed out toward the mountain knowing that they needed to be ready for the unexpected to happen. It was a mystery to them how she was able to convince a bear to fight for her.

White Cloud was feeling labor pains. She laid down on the blankets and closed her eyes. Peace came to her and held her hand, "I will be here with you during the birth of our son, my love. I am sorry for all that you have had to endure so far. But know this, our gift to our people will be a very helpful and important one. He will return what has been lost by many and open the hearts and souls of the ones who believe in good. You will be at my side soon, my love. Don't be afraid or worry about our son because together we will protect and guide him. Here on earth he will be protected and also have a teacher for awhile. They call him Buffalo Tear, and he is on his way to us now. He will help our son to understand his journey. When

Buffalo Tear comes, sit with him for a while so that he knows that his path is the correct one. He is pure of heart and soul and he too one day will be a guardian angel because of who he is inside."

White Cloud opened her eyes and to her amazement she was holding her son in her arms. Her baby son was lying on her chest, wrapped in a blanket. White Cloud was feeling wonderful and joyful inside, seeing her beautiful baby. Her son's eyes were as blue as the sky, and they sparkled with white light. His hair was also white in color.

I looked into my mother's eyes and smiled back to her. I could feel my mother's love for me as I laid in her arms, and I wanted her to feel my love for her. I then could feel the stress she felt, because she was thinking that she was going to have to leave me to keep me safe. It was hard for me to understand that, because I was way to little and young yet.

Then I see this man, "I am your father, and you are my son. You will never be alone. As you become older, you will not only be wiser, but you will also understand all things about life. There is much to learn even though you know the answers. As a human you have to experience all the different emotions in order to understand and control them in your inner self. When it is the correct time you will know what it is that you must do my son, always follow the truth and pass on your knowledge to others."

White Cloud then heard wild animals making loud calling sounds, but these sounds were not ones of sadness. They were calls of joy. The wolf, eagle, mountain lion, hawk, raven, coyote, bear, elk, deer, moose, and all the animals on the mountain were announcing her son's birth.

The warriors stopped in their tracks and looked at each

other. They couldn't believe what they were hearing. It seemed to them that the mountain in the distance was totally alive. With all the animals making noises, they knew that there had to be a reason for it but they had no idea what that reason was. A few of the warriors felt like turning around and leaving but they knew if they did they would be considered a disgrace to their people. When the animals stopped making their sounds, the warriors began moving again toward the mountain.

Buffalo Tear's village men were moving through the forest when suddenly they saw warriors ahead of them. Before any words were spoken they were attacked from their sides, front, and rear. They were completely surrounded and out numbered. Only three warriors from the village were able to escape the trap; Red Feather, Spotted Rabbit, and Running Elk. They knew that they had to return to the village to warn and prepare their people for another attack from this new enemy. They began to move slowly back down the mountain to their village people.

White Cloud woke up to the sound of something at the cave entrance. Her son was still asleep so she covered him with a blanket and moved slowly to the entranceway of the cave. When she peeked out she saw that the sound she heard was from the mountain animals gathering outside. She knew that they were there to watch over her son and that she had to leave the area to protect his location.

She looked back toward him and said, "I love you. Be strong."

When she turned to walk away she also thanked the animals for being his protectors. She hadn't gone very far when she realized that she wasn't alone. She continued to walk hoping that they would follow her awhile longer, before they decided to capture her.

The warriors kept their distance from her, to make sure that she had no others around her. After seeing what the bear did to the other search party, they wanted to be ready for anything. They followed and watched for a few minutes before they made their move at her.

A warrior called Badger stepped out in front of White Cloud and said, "We are here to take you back, witch." He drew his ax and knife along with the other warriors who surrounded her. "But you are going to go back in pieces because you have killed our fellow warriors."

As they closed in on her, White Cloud spoke, "I know how this will be. For those of you who survive and return to your village make sure you speak the truth of what has taken place on this quest. A few years from this day there will be a special warrior who will show you the correct path to follow in this world. My only hope is that some of you will listen and learn."

One of the warriors jumped at White Cloud and said, "You talk too much, you witch."

She was able to avoid the ax he had in hand, but the knife in his other hand, entered her side. Then there was a white flash from the sky and ground. Before the warriors could respond many lay dead on the ground. The warrior that attacked White Cloud was lying dead at the feet of a great white wolf and an eagle. They both stood beside White Cloud. Badger and a few others stood motionless because they knew if they even blinked an eye, they would also die.

White Cloud spoke, "If you put down your weapons and move away slowly you will live. You all can believe what you want too, but the truth is I am not a witch. I have been chosen by the ancient ones to fulfill a special need for our people. The child that was within me will be of great importance to all life here on Mother Earth. What is right and good will soon have a warrior protecting it. You all are still standing here because you also have been chosen to do what needs to be done."

Badger threw down his weapons and dropped to his knees, "I am sorry, White Cloud, for what has happened here. Inside I knew that something wasn't right, but I was unsure of what to believe, but now I do know. Let me help you because you are hurt."

"Yes, Badger, you can help, but not me because I will soon be with my love. Please go back to your people and tell them the truth of what you have witnessed. You will need to be strong and follow your inner self. I also hope that your fellow warriors do the same."

The other warriors threw down their knives and axes and dropped to their knees and spoke softly because they knew that White Cloud was not a witch, but a princess. They believed the words that she spoke about her being chosen and also her child, because of what they had witnessed so far.

"Yes Princess White Cloud. We have been wrong, but we swear on our lives to you that we will do all we can to correct this." They all said they were sorry for offending her and their ancestors at the same time.

White Cloud said, "Thank you," and stood up with great difficulty. "Go now, my people, and teach others what you have learned here today and be safe." The warriors all stood up and turned to walk away with new knowledge.

White Cloud tried to walk but she stumbled and fell back to the ground because she was very weak from her wound. The white wolf and eagle came to her side and spoke to her, "We will carry you to the place. Close your eyes and rest to regain your strength." When she closed her eyes she could feel their energy enfold around her. Then she felt like she was floating in the air up the mountain.

White Cloud opened her eyes and already knew the place. Peace had shown her the beautiful flower fields and the view of the valley below. She turned and looked up into Buffalo Tear's eyes.

Buffalo Tear now knew it was her time. "I will go to your son and do what is asked of me. Can I help you over to the ridge, Princess?"

"I can make it, my brother. Please go quickly to my son because he needs you now."

Buffalo Tear wrapped his arms around White Cloud's body and kissed her cheek and said, "Go with Peace. I will always honor and love you, my sister, for the rest of my days."

White Cloud then walked over to the edge of the ridge and stepped out onto a large boulder. Looking down she could see the river far below. She felt her heart stop. She looked up into the blue sky and stepped forward into the arms of Peace. White Cloud and Peace were holding hands as they floated above the ridge heading skyward. Buffalo Tear's eyes were filled with joy for them both as they waved to him. "Go to our son brother. You will be all that he needs. We will always be there for you and him. Thank you."

Buffalo Tear started running toward the oak tree cave. He couldn't wait to hold the newborn baby in his arms. As he approached the cave he became aware of all the wild animals about. He slowed to a walk so that the wild ones wouldn't feel that he was a threat to them or the little one.

At the cave's entrance stood a mountain lion, bear, and a wolf. When they saw Buffalo Tear they stepped aside to let him enter the cave. When he entered the cave, I began to cry. When I saw Buffalo Tear, I knew that my mother was not on this world anymore; it made me sad that I could no longer touch her. When he picked me up I could feel his energy; this man was full of love, respect and honesty. I tried to speak and tell him that I would give him the same. But being a newborn I could not speak the words so that he could understand, but by looking into his eyes I knew then that he did know what I was trying to tell him.

Buffalo Tear could sense that this baby was going to be a wonderful gift to all life. When he left the cave and passed by the animals he stopped for a moment to speak to them. "First I want to say thank you for watching over this child. Someday he will be a man who will bring about a change to mankind and also help to you. He is a wonder and a teacher to all life that will bring us all good. But for now he has to learn and see his purpose and understand his journey on Mother Earth. We all need to help. Thank you again my friends."

When Buffalo Tear walked out of the forest he noticed that his village was very still. As he started to cross the stream his people came running toward him because they were excited to see him alive.

One of the elder's spoke, "We were afraid that the enemy had taken you. Red Feather, Spotted Rabbit and Running Elk told us about the enemy tribe and that we should get ready for an attack by them."

Buffalo Tear then said, "They are gone and will not return to here again. The ones that survived know that this place is special and that they could never have control here."

Running Deer came to his side and asked, "Where did you find this baby?"

Buffalo Tear smiled and said, "Remember before I left to go to the mountain earlier I said that a special gift would be given to us. I now hold that gift and he will be in need of nourishment soon."

Looking at Running Deer, I realized that she had Morning Mist to feed, but she was the only one able to breast-feed me at this time.

"We are his people and we must accept this child as one of our own and not treat him as an outsider. We will teach this child and help raise him to adulthood. I will tell you this; in return, he will also teach and give more than any of us could ever imagine in return. He will also have help from the ones who have gone before us. Our people and world will prosper because he will help return the true meaning of life to us. And he will also help us to rediscover what has been lost when following your incorrect path."

Running Deer and Buffalo Tear walked back to her teepee. Red Feather, Running Deer's mate, was standing outside holding Morning Mist. He said, "It is good to see you have come home safe and it looks like we are going to have a new warrior."

Running Deer asked to take me inside so she could feed

me. "Here take him, but know this first, you will experience a wonderful feeling and we will talk about it later."

Buffalo Tear turned to Red Feather; "You had a terrible time on the mountain, my brother. Don't blame yourself for the loss of our people. Everything will work out all right. I know that it's hard to understand and that there will always be the question why. Our path will always have unavoidable distractions and you have to stay strong and stand into the light of goodness."

Red Feather shook his head yes and said, "I understand but it is difficult to accept."

Running Deer was riding her horse through the open plains. It was a wonderful feeling of beauty and freedom, but then she realized it was only in her mind because she sat breast-feeding the child. She could feel that this child was definitely a human who was different. When she first touched him she felt a burst of joy and comfort.

I stopped feeding and looked up into her eyes and thanked her. I tried to speak the words, but I couldn't because I was too young. I can't wait until I am old enough to be understood; it's frustrating not being able to communicate.

Running Deer took me to Buffalo Tear and said, "When he is in need, bring him to me please." She then touched her lips to my forehead and asked what my name was.

Buffalo Tears answered, "A name has not been chosen yet for him. I've decided to have a village council meeting to see if we can come up with one for him."

After a few weeks the village people sat together and discussed the village procedures. They would gather throughout the year to prepare for not only the changing of the seasons, but also to take care of any needs of their people. They could not decide on my name because they felt it was too soon. So for the time being I would be called "the young one" and that some day when the time was right I would be honored with the correct name.

When Badger and his warriors made it back to their village their chief and elders were disappointed that they came back empty handed. Badger and his men explained what had happened and how they felt about White Cloud. Dark Eye, the chief, and the village people had a hard time understanding and accepting the truth of what had happened.

Badger and his warriors remained loyal to White Cloud, remembering her words about being strong and following their inner guidance. They knew it was going to be difficult for their people to accept the truth, but they were going to stay the path no matter what the outcome.

Dark Eye and his council were very mad at Badger and his men but they knew that the village needed these warriors. Dark Eye and the council decided to just let it go and down play what had happened, to control it there own way, like they always had in the past.

Dark Eye was given that name when he was a child; he had a fight with another child who hit him with a pointed stone that caused the loss of his sight in that eye. When Dark Eye became older he had the chance to take revenge. One day on a hunting trip Dark Eye killed the man that had taken his eyesight. No one ever knew the truth in his village because he told them that a mountain lion had killed the warrior, and that Dark Eye in return had killed the cat.

# CHAPTER TWO

Six years had passed before the first test came to me. My physical body was still young but being who my true self was allowed me to do anything at anytime. This test wasn't going to be like the one that Buffalo Tear had when he was a young warrior or like any other warrior had ever experienced. Mother Earth and the mountain spirits were going to become a part of me during my experience. I had learned a lot from Buffalo Tear and from the people of his village. Dealing with the different emotions that one feels was sometimes confusing for me. All that is good will always out weigh the bad. Buffalo Tear had shown me how to follow my inner-self when I was unsure of an answer or what to do in a situation. He taught me how to look inward to find the truth.

Also at times when I would be meditating, I would be visited by my mother and father. They would help me to see the correct way and leave me with their love. It was always so beautiful and peaceful to be with them even if it was only for a short time. Buffalo Tear also showed me how the inner strength can over power the physical body. Pain is felt on the physical level but you can control it from the inner level. He taught me how to come to a higher awareness of the other strengths that everyone has, strengths that most others never come to realize they have.

I have learned how to know people for who they really are by seeing the energy that surrounds them. That energy is at times affected by other energy sources. Buffalo Tear has always spoken of being aware of good and bad, pure of heart and evil, to be aware that the conflict between good and evil will always exist, and that no matter how painful or long the struggle between the two becomes. In the very end only good will win the battle.

As I stood at my mentor's side by the sacred mountain, some other villagers came to us. Running Deer and Red Feather told me to enjoy the trip to the sacred mountain. I told Buffalo Tear and my people that I knew that I was going to have an experience with the wild animals on the mountain.

I could tell that they were worried about me being safe with them, so I said, "The wild ones and I are going to make contact with each other. There will be no harm felt between us. We will only feel joy in meeting each other."

I could tell that Buffalo Tear was still a little worried about me as he handed me a blanket and a knife that he took from his loincloth.

"You will be taught a lesson from Mother Earth this time. Make your way to the top of the mountain. There you will know when you are at the right place. Stay until you have been shown your new lesson of life. Remember all you have learned to this point because that knowledge will help guide you and protect you. I will return to this place everyday and wait for you to come back. Your people will also be waiting."

I then wrapped my arms around Buffalo Tear and gave him a hug because we both enjoyed the feelings of our love and energy for each other. This was an act that I had always done to my people to show them the respect and honor that I felt for them. They have also learned to do the same to each other, and I was always glad to see them do it because it was a good thing for them to learn.

I walked across the mountain stream to its other side and turned around and waved to my people. They weren't sure what I was doing, but Buffalo Tear did. So he told them, "Wave back to him because he is telling us that he loves us all and that he will return soon." So they all waved back to me.

As I entered the forest it wasn't long before I began to have visitors. With each new one I spoke the words, "I'm not here to harm you. I know that my people need some of you for food and clothing and I thank you for your sacrifice."

I was able to touch a rabbit, mouse, squirrel, turkey, fox, raven, doe and fawn, lynx, and a porcupine. Then I had a little surprise. Out of the brush came an animal that made me laugh. I sat down and he hurried over to me. It was a skunk; a beautiful and friendly one. Next came a raccoon, bear, elk, and hawk. The next two were the animals Buffalo Tear had told me were very special to me: the eagle and wolf. But they were not pure white. The eagle was a golden eagle and the wolf was a beautiful silver color. As I touched them I knew right away that they were definitely my totems. Your animal totems can give you internal strength, protection, and help heal your physical body. I could feel their strength and devotion to me. In return I wanted them to feel my respect, honor, and love for them. We are as one and always will be because we will always protect each other forever. After meeting my totems and the other animals of the wild I felt much joy and peace in my heart.

As I continued up the mountain my totems stayed with me. The eagle flying overhead and the wolf near my side. The wolf suddenly stopped and began to growl deeply. Looking forward I could see a mountain lion approaching. He walked proudly toward me, but when he spotted the wolf he slowed down and lowered his head and tail. My totems and I could tell by his body language that all he wanted to do was to say, "Hello." The wolf sat down and the eagle landed in a tree over head.

I spoke to the mountain lion, "It is all right, my friend." When he came to me, I touched his head with my hand. I could feel him relax and I could feel his excitement about being a part of my new found friends.

As I continued to walk to the mountaintop, I could tell that this place on Mother Earth was a very special location. Everything about it was beautiful; the wild life, plants, scenery, sky, clouds, and sun. As I walked through a field of flowers at the mountaintop, I followed my inner instinct to the correct spot.

Then in front of me appeared a bright light from the sky to the earth and standing inside it was my parents. I was so happy to see them and as I reached out to them with my arms. My body was enfolded with the light. For the first time in years I was able to hold them physically close to me. The love that flowed between us was so wonderful that I wanted to stay with them. I didn't want to release them from my arms even though I knew that I would have to. They wanted me to look up into their eyes, but I couldn't yet because I knew what they were going to say to me. I just needed to hold them both for a little longer and they agreed to my need. While holding each other close we were united as one. I could feel their needs as they could feel mine. No words were spoken aloud. Our communication was done by touch only. They wanted me to be safe, courageous, strong, and to always follow my true inner soul.

My father began speaking, "You will have many difficult challenges to face and that some mistakes might be made. And when you realize the mistakes, please correct them and the outcome will always be for the good."

My mother then said, "You will know, son, what is right because you are the white light of goodness and truth. Your soul will always do and follow the correct path, and as a human you have to be able to allow that to be. There are a lot of emotions that come into play when making decisions. The most important one of them all is the one we feel right now and we will forever: love."

"I understand, Mother and Father. I also know that you will always be there for me. I will return to our people and help guide them the best I can to the light. I realize that I'm still very young, but that my purpose here on Mother Earth is for goodness of all life. I will do my best for our Creator and you, my parents. I will always strive to be the best I can be and when I do make a mistake I hope to realize it, so that I can correct it."

All of a sudden I felt something touch my shoulders and back. My Mother and Father both smiled and said. "You have been given a sign of symbols for our people to see and know that you are very special and important, individual for all life on Mother Earth. Remain strong, son. Return to our people and continue to grow and learn because your destiny is one of great importance to all life."

The sun was just coming up in the eastern skyline. It was so beautiful, the sights, sound, smell, and touch of Mother Earth. It was time to go to my village, so as I began to walk down the mountain my animal friends started to return to my side. I enjoyed their company all through the forest. It was fun to see them trying to communicate with each other. Just before we reached the stream I stopped for a moment and said farewell to my friends and told them to be safe. They all said goodbye in their own voices, which made quite a lot of noise. We laughed and went our separate ways.

When I reached the stream bank, Buffalo Tear was standing across from me. By the time I waded across it some of the other villagers were standing with him.

"Welcome home, Young One." Running Deer asked if I was hungry and if I needed to rest.

I said, "No, I feel fine. Why do you ask me this?"

"Because you have been gone for three days and we all were getting worried about you." I looked at Buffalo Tear, together we both smiled; I was surprised to hear three days.

"You're right, Running Deer. I could eat something." After the meal I hugged and thanked Running Deer not only for the food, but also for being like a mother to me. Buffalo Tear and I made our way back to our place. It was different than all the others because he meant a lot to his people. They lived in tepees. Buffalo Tear was located at the center of the village in a wigwam that was in a circular shape made of tree limbs, grass, rocks, and all items from Mother Earth. Painted symbols of the sun, earth, wind, and water were painted above the entrance. The paint colors were made of materials from Mother Earth and animals.

Once inside, we sat down together inside another circle which was made up of many different colored stones that were crystals. We talked about my experience on the mountain and about what I needed to do as a young learner, how to be observant and to be careful on making any judgments. Buffalo Tear told me that deception is a difficult thing to see, but it cannot ever hide from the true truth.

"For the time being, I want you to understand why you must do this."

Buffalo Tear then handed me a leather shirt that Running Deer had made for me. "I want you to wear this at all times when you are around our people. The reason for this is because the markings on your back may scare and confuse some of them. I want you to be able to be just an ordinary child in their eyes for now, so that you can see what needs to be corrected in time. Yes, we are hiding the truth for the time being. There are three reasons for this. One reason is that you are not old enough or ready, because you have much more to learn. Two, our people are not going to let a young one teach them the right path. And three, in time you will know when it is your time to show them what has been lost and that it needs to be returned in order for all to live a life of goodness and true beauty."

"Buffalo Tear, what is on my back and why can't I tell what it is? I remember when my parents said that I had been given a sign for our people to help them to understand me."

"You can see it if you concentrate on it. But I will tell you this; there is a warrior with his totems, a wolf and eagle, and they are standing in the light of truth. And you, Young One, someday will be known as the Warrior of Truth. The day that our people name you that name, will be a new beginning for all life. So for now, our secret is your true name so that you can continue your learning among all life. In the years to come your knowledge and wisdom and inner soul will become our people's light of goodness and hope for a better way of life on Mother Earth."

Red Feather called out to Buffalo Tear, "We have a messenger from a distant village who needs to speak to you. Can we enter?"

"Yes, you may enter," Buffalo Tear then touched my face and looked deep into my eyes. He didn't speak a word, but I knew what he was thinking, "I love you, Warrior of Truth. Go now to our people for there is still much to see and learn. Be who you are and remain strong." As I went by Red Feather and the messenger I knew what he had come here for. It was because he and his people needed our help.

"Come, sit down, Sparrow." A look of amazement came upon the messenger's face. "I did speak your correct name I hope?"

"Yes, half of it, "I'm known as Sparrow Hawk." Buffalo Tear and Red Feather began to laugh and then Sparrow Hawk joined in too. "I'm honored to sit at your side, Buffalo Tear. I have heard many stories about you and your deeds. Some I thought were just over exaggerated, but not anymore," they all laughed together again.

"You have come to ask if you and your people may join our village. You are all welcome here. We will help your people to regain their strength." Sparrow Hawk was again amazed at how Buffalo Tear had the insight to the needs of people.

Sparrow Hawk then spoke, "I will do whatever you ask

of me and so will my people because you are a very special leader. My people, what's left of them, and I thank you for your generosity."

Buffalo Tear then asked Sparrow Hawk to tell him about the happenings that placed his village in such a poor state. Sparrow Hawk lowered his head and said, "It all started four summers ago. Men dressed with metal on their bodies visited our village and some were riding horses. In the beginning all they wanted was to trade things for food and information about the land. When our food supply started to get low, we asked for their help. Instead, they misused our women and men and stole from us. They began to destroy our land by building large walls and wooden buildings. When we decided to move the village they attacked us and killed many of our people. Only a few of us escaped. After a few days on the run we met up with another village that had been destroyed by the same people. We traveled together knowing that we could defend ourselves better against them. Heading north, we came to a large open sand area that had very little water and food. After crossing it, we started to come across more people with white skin and they also wanted to fight us. They used weapons called guns. They made a loud bang and what ever they were pointed at, would be hurt or killed.

"We finally came to a village that let us stay with them, but they also had a lot of problems. We fought many battles; some against the white men and some against our own people. There were some battles that I fought in where I discovered some of our people from a different tribe fighting along side the whites. I didn't understand or like what was happening and I still don't to this day. With all the fighting along with the everyday struggle for life, the village became weak to the point of total destruction. I gathered all who wanted to leave for survival and lead them away to the east, getting as far away as possible from that evil. I had been told many stories about you, Buffalo Tear, and every one of them was about your strength to bring good to our people. So my search for you began and now that we are here I realize that our people are in good hands."

Buffalo Tear smiled and said, "Yes, I'm here to help our people and so are you and all those who are true of heart. We stand for good and will always confront the evil that exists. You are not in my hands, but in the hands of the Creator. It is He that we owe ourselves to. Always honor and respect all that is his."

The three of them stood up and walked outside to see the sunset behind the sacred mountain. The beauty was breath taking. The ray of bright white light encircling the mountain with blue sky and all the colors of Mother Earth was a beautiful gift of sight.

Within a short period of time the days started to get cooler and the nights were longer. When the sun came up in the morning there would be a heavy frost on the ground. The winter would soon arrive; our village would need to be prepared for the winter season. With the growth of our village, one of the biggest problems was the food supply.

I had made a few new friends, some were older, and from the new people in our village. One day I was asked to go hunting with some of the young warriors. They asked me because they knew that my accuracy with a bow and arrow was amazing. I could even outshoot the adult warriors when we practiced with targets. My only concern was that hitting a target was not the same as shooting a live animal and I couldn't tell them this. I love, respect, and honor the wild animals. How was I going to take their lives? I knew that meat was needed for our people to survive. I just wasn't sure how I was going to do this task. I knew that I was about to learn something important so I agreed to go, as long as we did not go to the mountain to hunt. In the early morning we headed out to the south, which was a low land area that was swampy. When we entered the wet lands, our group split up into pairs and headed off in different directions. We were all suppose to meet back together before sun down.

My partner was a young warrior that was older then I was and who was called Beaver Tooth. He acquired his name because he liked to swim with the beavers and one day he followed a beaver into his stick house. Once he was inside he became trapped so he had to dig his way out through the top. When he popped his head out he had a beavers stick in his mouth. His friend said that he didn't dig his way out, but that he chewed his way out so he became known as Beaver Tooth.

We hadn't gone very far before we came across fresh deer tracks. They were close so we started to track them down. Beaver Tooth was trying hard but he was making many mistakes. The first one was that he didn't notice that the deer that we were tracking had a young one with them. I could tell that there was at least a mother doe and fawn, a young buck, and three older deer. Two of them were bucks with the third one being a very old female deer. I decided to let him do the tracking because if he continued, I felt that the deer would be safe. But up ahead I could see them standing watching us. They blended in perfect with the swampy trees, brush, and dry grass. Beaver Tooth didn't see them yet so he kept on moving forward. When they jumped and started running I smiled to myself inside.

Beaver Tooth turned to me and whispered, "Lets circle around and try to cut them off." Looking over his shoulder I could see the old one coming toward us. I knew right away what she was doing. I tried to tell her to stop and go back, but she told me that she had had enough of this life and that she wanted to help by giving herself freely so that others could survive; our people and her species.

Beaver Tooth realized that I was looking at something so he turned around and drew back his bow and arrow and waited for a clear shot. I didn't want this to happen so I touched his back and asked him not to shoot, but he did. It was a clean shot; the arrow entered her heart and she fell to the ground.

I ran to her and held her head. Looking into her eyes I could feel that she wanted me not to be upset with Beaver Tooth. *Some things are meant to be and can not be changed. I will be in a much better place. My journey here is over and my sacrifice will feed your people and allow my species to be safe and stronger with out me. Please complete the ceremony by accepting my sacrifice, release my spirit to the Creator with the prayers of gratitude you have learned.*

I thanked her for sacrificing her life for my people and protecting the other deer. I pulled out my medicine pouch, which was always at my side tied to the sheath of my knife. I took a pinch of the sacred herbs that the pouch contained. While still holding the doe's head, I put the herbs into each nostril, her eyes, and ears, so that her senses would be cleansed, and her spirit's journey would be blessed. I placed her head onto the ground and sprinkled some herbs around her body, and on Mother Earth, to give thanks to the plants that the deer had eaten during her time on Mother Earth. I spoke aloud my people's prayer of gratitude, "I thank you, wild one, for your gift of life so my people may live. Everything that you have given us will be accepted with respect and honor, food, tools, and clothing. Release your soul to the Great Spirit; go to our Creator for a new beginning." Her body then went still because her soul had left her.

Beaver Tooth was about to begin to butcher her, but I yelled, "Wait, you must first thank her for what she has given. Respect and honor her life." He looked at me in a strange way because he did not completely understand what I was saying to him. I was about to explain it to him, but we heard some of our warriors screaming for help. Something terrible was happening so we started running in the direction of the yelling. As we got closer I started to get this feeling of a bad energy source emanating not far in front of us.

"Beaver Tooth, stop. We must go slow and be very cautious because there is evil waiting near."

Beaver Tooth then said, "What is wrong with you? We must help them. Come on!" Beaver Tooth started to run again, but only a short distance because a huge brown bear ran into his left side, knocking him to the ground. Two other young warriors came running over, but they had already encountered the bear because there were claw and teeth marks on their bodies. The bear rose up on his hind legs and was about to strike a blow to Beaver Tooth when I jumped onto his back and wrapped my arms around his neck to cut off his air supply.

As soon as I touched him I could feel his rage and hatred for people. He wanted us all to be dead. Beaver Tooth got back up and found his bow. He and the other two warriors were ready to shoot but they were afraid that an arrow might hit me. The bear dropped to the ground and started to roll around to loosen up my grip on him. He rolled over close to them and made a big swiping blow with his left front paw knocking all three of them over and onto the ground. He then rolled over onto one of them clawing him apart, killing him.

I knew that I had to stop this, so I jumped off his back and reached out for a bow that was on the ground. I picked up the bow, but it had no arrows with it. The bear now turned to attack Beaver Tooth and the other warrior. I saw a quiver of arrows by the dead warrior's side. So I picked them up and placed an arrow on the bow and drew it back as he began attacking the other two. I knew that if I was to save them my shot had to be not only accurate, but one that would stop him. As I aimed the arrow at the center of the back of his neck, the bear killed the warrior who was with Beaver Tooth.

He then attacked Beaver Tooth, so I shot the arrow at the bear; he fell motionless on top of Beaver Tooth. The bear was still breathing, but he was unable to move any part of his body because the arrow was imbedded in his backbone.

Beaver Tooth was still alive, but he could not get the bear off of him. It was very difficult to remove the bear off of Beaver Tooth, but I did it. Beaver Tooth was hurt badly from the bear's attack; his wounds were deep and bleeding a lot. I knew that I needed to stop the bleeding quickly or he too would die as well. I took some of our clothing and wrapped it around his deep wounds with tight pressure. I started a fire and when the end of a hardwood branch glowed red from the heat I touched the bad open wounds on Beaver Tooth with it. The bleeding stopped, but I knew that his wounds would take some time to heal and that he would be left with many large scars.

Looking back over at the bear I could see him still breathing and still unable to move any part of his body. I could still feel the evil in him along with his hatred toward us. I wasn't sure why these feelings in him were so strong. Was it something during his life that my people had done to him and his kind or was it just born into him? All I knew that mattered now was what needed to be done. I could not let him lie there and suffer until his death, so I walked over to him with a knife in hand.

I looked into his eyes and spoke, "I know you're evil, but the way it controls you I am not sure about. What you have done to my people and to other lives was wrong and I will not take your life because of that. But I can stop your suffering and release your soul of this evil, go in peace."

I placed my hand over his eyes and cut open his throat and released him from this life. His life was the first one that I took and it was an action that I did not like.

I went back to Beaver Tooth and kneeled at his side and he reached up and touched my arm. "Thank you. Young One. I was stupid for not listening to you and allowing all this to happen. Are there any others who made it?"

"I'm not sure. I will have to go looking for them, but you need to rest and stay here. I will be back shortly."

I started to back-track the bear's path hoping to find some of the ones in our hunting party from our village. After a short period of time I came across where they had encountered the bear. There were four mutilated warriors. I continued to search some more and hadn't gone very far when I felt the presence of something I wasn't sure of. So I hid in some thick brush and waited to see what it was.

Two men were riding on horses and they were dressed with

metal armor on there upper bodies. I had heard about these white men from Sparrow Hawks people in my village. As they came closer, the feeling I had became stronger. They wanted control over this new land and to gather all of its treasures. When they passed by me I could hear them talking and they spoke in a different language, but I understood it and knew what they were looking for. They had heard the fighting of the bear and my people and they were searching for the location of it. I needed to get back to Beaver Tooth before they discovered him, but the only problem now was they were headed straight toward him. I had to come up with a plan to change their direction of travel.

I stood up and started running away making a lot of noise so that they would follow me. I glanced back to see if they were coming. They were just turning the horses toward me to begin chasing after me. I knew that I could loose them, but first I needed to lead them a long distance away from Beaver Tooth. When I figured that I had gone far enough I started to look for a way to lose them. To my right side I could see an area that was an open wetland with very tall grass. So I headed toward it, ran into the tall grass and ducked down low. When they entered the grass, I circled back around them so I could get back to Beaver Tooth.

I made it back to Beaver Tooth just before sun down. I helped him to his feet, but he was still too weak to go very far. We had to find a safe place for him to rest for the night. I also knew that the two who were chasing me would return to this area because they couldn't find me. If they discovered this place they would figure out that there were two of us and that one was wounded. I helped Beaver Tooth to walk because he was still very weak from his wounds. We headed back toward the swampy wetland area slowly. When we made it there we located a place to stay and rest for the night.

Just before morning I could smell smoke from a campfire. There was a freshly fallen tree near so I placed Beaver Tooth underneath it and covered him with its branches and leaves. "Stay here and rest some more. I will return shortly with some food. It will help you regain your strength because we cannot stay here for too long."

I went back over to where I could smell the smoke again and went in that direction. I soon found the camp of the two men that had been after us. The only problem now was that there were about twenty too thirty of them, with some Indians. After observing them for awhile I figured out that my people were there as guides to help them because this land was foreign to them. Next to one of the campfires were the hides of a deer and bear and the meat from them was being smoked and cooked. I had to figure out a way to get some of that food for Beaver Tooth. Then I got an idea.

A bunch of their horses were tied up together at a tree. I needed to get over to them and set them free to make a diversion so I could sneak in and gather up some meat. I worked my way over to the horses and cut the rope and slapped a horse on his side. When he jumped and started running so did the others. A few went running through the camp and others went in different directions. The white men started shouting and running after them. I waited until they were all busy chasing the horses around before I walked over to the meat and placed it into a bag that was on the ground, I then started to walk away.

One of the Indian guides stepped out in front of me and asked, "What are you doing?"

"I am taking back what my people fought and died for."

He stepped aside and said, "Get out of here now because you have caused a lot of trouble here."

I started to run, but not in the direction of Beaver Tooth because I felt that he was not being completely good. After a ways I found a place to hide the food in a hollow tree and then headed off toward Beaver Tooth. I was almost to him when I knew that I had to stop.

Then I yelled out, "All right I will go no further and you will not find my friend. So come and take me back to your camp." I spoke loud enough so that Beaver Tooth could hear what was going on.

"You who let me go at the camp. Come to me, along with the rest of you." He came from my left side and behind him were three more of my people along with some of the white men.

He then asked, "Where is your friend because we know that he is hurt and maybe we can help him?"

"He does not need your help. He is in enough pain, and I will not let him suffer for anything I have done."

"Okay, if that's the way you want it, maybe I should just beat it out of you or let the whites handle this."

"You only want to be able to capture both of us so you can ask for extra rewards from these white people. You also feel that it will show them exactly how good your tracking ability is."

He walked over to me closer and grabbed me by the shoulder. "Who are you and how do you know what I am thinking?"

I only looked straight into his eyes and said nothing to him because I could read him so easily. At the moment he was very confused about his actions because he wasn't completely sure that he was doing the right thing. He liked the rewards and recognition that the whites gave to him for his deeds, but he did not trust any of them. He knew what they had done in the past to his own people for information about things. Some were tortured and others killed.

His name then came to me, "Fox, you are only a slave to these people. You have lost your true self. Material things, bringing attention to you for your ego, wanting a better life, is not totally bad. But the way you are going about it is. You know this and you also know that you are the only one who can make it right."

Fox then let go of me and turned and walked away, but then the white men put my arms behind me and tied my hands together and took me back to their camp. They brought me over to their leader and he started to ask me questions.

"Where do you come from? What are you doing here? And where are the rest of your people? Look, boy, you better answer me now. You tried to steal our horses and food and if you do not speak, I will make you." He hit my face with his fist, but I stood strong and looked at him. He hit me again in the face and then punched my stomach a few times. When I dropped to my knees he started to kick me. His men started laughing. He stopped hitting me and said, "Now talk to me, if you're awake."

I sat up and then stood up straight in front of him. All the laughter stopped because his men knew that I was defying him. I stood up strong with my inner strength. I had blood on my face and clothes. He then grabbed my shirt and ripped it off me.

"Take him to that tree over there and tie him up because

he is going to get a whipping from me." He walked over to the tree as they were tying my arms above my head. "I told you to answer me and now you will or you will die."

I said nothing and closed my eyes; White Cloud and Peace came to me. "You will not die, son. Be strong and follow your inner feelings and don't give up on your people."

I could feel the whip striking my body. My legs, arms, and back were in pain, but I was able to direct the pain away. Fox and other warriors had gathered around. Fox started yelling at the leader to stop. But the white men's leader only glanced back at Fox with a grin on his face. He raised his arm to strike me with the whip again. But instead an arrow hit him in his chest and he dropped to the ground.

The arrow came from a warrior's bow that realized who I was, from what was now visible on my back because of the whipping. He was much older now, but he remembered the woman who had turned his life around. He tried to teach his son, Fox, what he had learned and hoped that someday he too would also follow the right path.

The white men brought their guns up and shot him as he was walking over to his son. Fox and the other warriors now attacked the whites. During the fighting, Fox made his way over to his father.

"Son, remember the story I told you about a woman called White Cloud. That young warrior is her son because of the markings on his back. The wolf and eagle are signs on his back that told me who he is. Help him, look and listen to him, because he will help you discover your true self."

Badger closed his eyes and Fox hugged him and said, "Yes, Father. I will learn because I have just learned an important thing. I will miss you, my father, and I will always honor and respect you."

Fox ran over to me and as he reached up to cut the rope that held me to the tree he stared at my back. Even with my back all bloody he could see the wolf and eagle. He hadn't seen it before the whipping but it was now etched onto my back by the whip. He also noticed that there was something else between them, but it was too hard to see because of all the swelling of my back. When he cut the rope I fell to my knees and he helped me to stand back up.

The fighting was still going on, but I went over to his father and touched him. "Thank you, Badger. My parents will help you on your new journey."

Fox, with his eyes wet with tears said, "Come, we must leave here because more of the whites are coming." He started yelling for his warriors to join us and when they all came we left the camp area. I felt weak, but I told Fox that I had to get my friend who should be waiting.

When I found the place he was at I called out to him, "Beaver Tooth, you can come out. It is all right." He crawled out from under the brush and came over and asked, "What happened and who are these warriors with you?"

"I can't explain it right now because we have to move quickly to lose the whites so we can return home."

Fox said, "Lets go to the big water. We can lose them there. I have some canoes hidden that the whites do not know about."

"All right, but you and your warriors go ahead and we will follow," I said that as a test for Fox.

He passed it when he said, "I will not let you follow us

because you both are hurt and weak. We must all travel together for safety and strength."

I smiled and said, "Good idea." By the time we made it to the water my body was totally exhausted so I went to sleep in the canoe while they paddled away from shore.

When I woke up I was feeling wet and cold because Mother Earth was bringing us snow. Winters were a difficult time, so we needed to get to shore and make a shelter for warmth and protection from the storm. By the time we reached solid ground, the snow was over a foot deep. We had a very hard time moving around in it. So we decided to pile the canoes together and gathered up some pine tree limbs for a temporary shelter. The snow continued for two more days before it stopped. During the two days we talked about what we needed to do for our survival.

Fox knew of a village a few days away that we might be able to stay at. The only problem was that this village was the village his father once lived in, but he left it because of his experience with White Cloud.

Badger, along with the warriors who met my mother, wanted nothing to do with the chief of the village anymore. After they left, their chief sent some warriors out to bring them back. Badger's woman, who was close to giving birth, and a few others were captured and returned to the village. Badger and his young son and a few others had to find a new area to live.

Fox said that chief Dark Eye was not a good leader and that he brought a lot of bad to the village people. His only hope was that maybe by now someone else was in charge. I suggested that we go there, but once we arrived I would enter the village to see if it was safe for the rest of them. Fox and the other warriors looked at me with wonder in their eyes.

"You don't even know us and yet you are willing to do this, which could be dangerous."

"Yes, I am willing to do this because I do know you and you are my people. I am here for a reason just as all of you are, and it is important that you discover your true self and follow the correct path. Your father did and so did many others from his village. It may take some time, but once you have it in plain view you will know your path and you will follow it with strength."

Beaver Tooth reached out and touched my shoulder and said, "You, my friend, are not to be called Young One anymore. We, who are here with you this day, know and have seen your strength and wisdom. All my life, and I think these warriors agree to, that all their lives, they too have not seen anyone who is such a wonder. You are a true warrior, one for good and also our people. You have always battled the bad and brought out the good that is hidden or lost in us. I ask you, Fox, and my brothers here, what do you think about him?"

"He is not the Young One anymore. How about the True One or better yet the Warrior of Truth." They all agreed Warrior of Truth was a name fitting for me.

I sat up straight with a smile on my face and told them that I was honored by my people and I thanked them. "I will always be true to you all," and I reached out to touch them all with my hands. As I finished, we all heard both the wolf and eagle cry out into the night with great loudness. I then said to them, "That is our ancestors also thanking you and respecting your decision. We are as one and always will be."

Fox, Beaver Tooth, Falcon, White Tail, Crow, Red Hawk,

Bobcat, White Owl, Bear Foot, Caribou Ear, Moose Rib all said in unison, "Together we will help our people with their struggles against all that is not good. We must always honor and respect all that our Creator has given us along with each other. One is not better than another. We are all equal. We walk together now and in time we will again walk together, but in the light of the ones before us."

"Come let's form a circle," and as we did I reached my hand into the center and all the others did too, and together we touched hands. Together we made a promise to protect each other, our people, and do our best to always defeat the evil in this world. A bright light came through the top of our shelter and encircled our hands. "Our ancestors have given us another sign. They are telling us that they are glad to see twelve warriors helping to do good things for their people." We all had a red mark across the top of our right hands to show our connection to each other and our strength of togetherness.

"All right my brothers, let us continue our journey and go find the village and do what we must, to make things right for our people and life on Mother Earth."

After four days of travel in the cold and deep snow, we came to a village. Fox said, "This is not the village of Dark Eye, but it is close to it. I know because the area does look familiar to me."

While looking at the village, my attention was drawn to a mud hut at the far end. "Fox, I am going to circle around to that mud hut over there and see if I can locate anyone friendly."

"Wait a minute. This must be a part of Dark Eye's village. I recognize that mud hut over there. That place was the home of the village healer. The people thought she was a witch, but Badger said that she was not. At one time there was an old one, and a young one. They both always helped our people, but Dark Eye made them stay away from the village. My father said that Dark Eye was afraid of them because they were always against his leadership."

"Fox, did Badger tell you who the young one was?"

"Yes, my father did. He always honored and respected her. He called her White Cloud."

We both smiled because we both knew that we had returned to a place that needed us. "I'll make my way over to the hut. If you go into the village from here be careful and remain alert for any danger."

As I was about to head out toward the hut, we could hear a person screaming in great pain. The sound came from a short distance away. Someone was being hurt in the main part of the village.

I continued to make my way around to the hut. As I was moving, I noticed some villagers staying in this small area; I felt that these were villagers who were not allowed to live in the main village. I stopped at the entrance to the mud hut and asked to enter. There was silence for a moment, and then a woman said, "Yes, come in."

The woman seemed wary of me. She was not sure who I was or why I was there. She, too, was the village healer just like all the ones before her. She was still an outcast, along with the others in her small village.

She then asked, "What can I do for you? Because you don't look sick, but you do look like you have been hurt."

I gave her a smile and said, "I am not hurt and I am not

here to hurt you. I can feel your fear and also the pain you have suffered here before."

She looked at me with wonder because she had two questions to ask. She was afraid to ask them because she didn't want to get hurt. The first question was how did I know of her pain? The second was, she wondered if I was trying to trick her and lie to her so that Dark Eye could hurt her again to show her people his control over her. Because of all that she had been through she felt that she could not trust anyone anymore.

Her name came to me, but before I said it, I needed to convince her that I would never cause her any harm. If I called her by her name or answered her silent questions right now. I wondered, if that would help her to understand that she would be safe with me. Or if it would just raise more doubt within her.

I thought maybe I should just turn around and leave but then it came to me that nothing good had been accomplished here yet.

I stepped closer to her and looked deep into her eyes and said, "I understand that it is hard but you can trust me." I reached out my hands to her. "If you touch my hands with yours, and open your inner-self to me, you will know that I am not here to hurt you, Lily. Allow the good in you to show you the truth."

I could feel the fear in her when I spoke her name so I went to my knees, but still held out my hands to her.

"You have to be strong and know you are doing what is right." She reached down with her hands and touched mine. I then could feel the fear and doubt leave her. Without any words spoken I answered her two questions.

After a few moments, with tears in her eyes she asked, "Where have you been? You are needed by so many of us. Why have we had to wait so long?"

"Our Creator is the one who determines when the time is correct. What is needed has always been with us since the beginning and it will be forever. The only problem is that for some it has been lost, but it can be rediscovered. For the ones that are completely controlled by evil, they may never see the light. Our purpose is to open the hearts, minds, and souls of those who are lost. This good will always bring the light of truth to their side."

Lily then said, "You must be careful here because the chief of this village is very bad."

"I already know about Dark Eye, and so do my brothers. We are in need of food and shelter to regain our physical strength.

"Where are your brothers and how many are there?"

"They are close and being very cautious because they know that Dark Eye is treacherous."

"The ones who live here with me are not allowed to enter the main village without Dark Eye's permission. We are only allowed to be workers for the main village people. I think that some are still loyal to the chief. So it won't be long before he knows that you are here and that could mean big trouble for us all."

"Lily, I understand what you are saying. This is only another step along the path of my journey. I will follow my path with strength."

Fox entered the hut and spoke, "We must leave, Dark Eye's warriors are surrounding this encampment."

"Fox, you and the others leave and go east until you come

to a river with a waterfall. Follow the river to the open plains and in the distance you will be able to see a mountain. Go toward the mountain. When you get to it, be respectful to all life there because it is sacred ground for our ancestors and us. There will be a village on the other side of the mountain. You will be greeted and accepted with respect from my people. Please tell Buffalo Tear that I have a new name and that I will see him soon. Thank him for me, for giving me his teaching. Ask him to please remain strong with our people until my return."

"I can't leave you here alone."

"Fox, please listen. You must do this. I will be all right. Your destiny is one of great importance. If you remain here, evil influence could change your true journey. Go now, my brother, and be safe."

"I will do what you ask of me, Warrior of Truth. I look forward to seeing you soon."

When he left, I looked to Lily and said, "I must make Dark Eye's warriors come to me. That will give my brothers a chance to escape from here."

"They may try to kill you if you fight them."

"I will fight them but I will fight them in a way they have never experienced before." I went outside the hut and stood on a large boulder. I then yelled out, "Warriors of Dark Eye, I believe you are looking for me. Come here. I will see just how strong you all are unless you're afraid of me." I knew my words would make them come and challenge me.

They all came over to me. Some had their bow and arrows at full draw, ready to shoot me.

The lead warrior spoke, "You are a young fool to challenge any of us. I think we should just kill you now."

"If you think you can, then try. I will fight back and some of you may get hurt. But I will not kill anyone."

He laughed and said, "You are so stupid." Then he pointed to one of the warriors who had his bow drawn and said, "Shoot him."

When the warrior released the arrow, I turned to the side, and the arrow missed me. He then pointed to another warrior and when he shot, I turned again and his arrow also missed me. Now the people who were in the camp were watching what was happening.

"Not bad, but let's see if you can evade this." He brought his bow up and told three others to shoot when he did. When he released his arrow the others did the same. They were all amazed when I leaped off the boulder toward them. When my feet touched the ground I stood up straight in front of their leader. In my hands I held the four arrows that they had shot at me. I pushed two arrows into the leader's right shoulder, and the other two, into his left shoulder. I only allowed the arrows to penetrate his skin and not go deep into his body.

"I told you that you might get hurt and that I would not kill anyone. The pain that you feel is only miner compared to the pain you have caused to others. You have let Dark Eye's bad ways influence and control your true self and life around you."

As he sat down on the ground he yelled out, "Who are you?" The other warriors were not sure what to do after witnessing what just happened.

"He will be all right. His wounds are not serious. I was only defending myself against your bad doings. You all are not true evil; it is only the way you have adapted too for your survival here. Some of you will finally see the wrong and some will not yet. Everyone's true soul is good, but you can become blind to that good when you do things and follow others who believe that they want control and power over life. Also when hatred, revenge, along with other wrong emotions over powers you, things are only done the wrong way. And if you continue to follow that path your true soul will not be a part of you physically on Mother Earth because the wrong and evil has over powered your true soul. When your time on Mother Earth is over you will only see the white light if you have any remains of your true and pure soul left within you. A new beginning will always be there for those whose true soul exists. But the wrong and evil will not ever be allowed to go into the white light. It must be stopped now in order for your true self to have strength to follow the correct path here on Mother Earth, and to have a new beginning in time."

As I said that, a warrior ran to me with a knife. He intended to kill me. I knew he would try because I could see the evil in his eyes when he stopped in front of me. I grabbed his arm and broke it. The knife fell out of his hand to the ground. I picked it up and looked at him. Everyone knew that I could kill him. Instead, I broke the knife in half, and threw it away because I could feel all the pain that it had caused to our people.

"You, warriors, should return to your chief now. Tell him I will not leave this camp if you are planning on hurting the people here. Your chief will want me dead because of who he is and also because of who I am. I will not let him destroy the innocent and good of our people anymore. All of you know right from wrong, but you're not doing what is right. You are living your lives under this chief's ruling. I understand that in order for your survival here you have had to do things that you really didn't want to do. But the more wrong that is done, the stronger evil becomes, and the worse things become for you."

I turned to the warrior who still had the four arrows in his shoulders. "I will remove these arrows from you, but you will again feel some pain. And again, it will be nothing compared to what you have given to others."

I removed the arrows from his shoulders. His warriors helped him to his feet and they started to walk back toward the main village.

Lily touched my hand and said, "You have just opened their eyes and my only hope is that they stay open now."

"Lily, I am concerned about you and your people because if I leave here now, Dark Eye will destroy you all because of me. If I remain here, he will return here and try to kill me and everyone here. You know that I have to go to Dark Eye and face him there to keep everyone safe here. I am not afraid of him, but I am afraid of what he can and will do to our people."

The people in camp had gather around us. An old warrior said, "If you go to Dark Eye, we will go with you. What we have seen and heard today is the sign that we have been waiting for for many years. Some of us have tried to stop Dark Eye before, but many have died in their quest. There has never been a warrior that's faced him with your strength, courage and true heart like yours. In my years I have made many mistakes as most of us here have, and before my time is over I want to cleanse my soul and hope for forgiveness. I will follow you and do what ever you ask of me and so will others."

"Please wait. My people. I understand how you feel, but this is going to be very dangerous and you all have been hurt enough by this man. I honor you all for your courage, but I don't want any of you to feel pain from him again."

"We will if anything happens to you. Please let us be a part of this because we owe this to ourselves, as well as our people." I smiled because I knew that their true selves had returned to them all now, after their times of difficultly living at this village. I knew that I needed to do everything that I could to keep them safe from Dark Eye and his evil ways.

When the warriors entered the main village, the women, children, and other villagers, followed them to Dark Eye's tepee. Dark Eye was outside, watching the warriors approach. He was angry to see there were no captives and that the leader was wounded. When he heard that one man had defeated them and how he had defeated them, Dark Eye became enraged with anger. The village people started talking quietly among themselves.

Dark Eye walked over to the wounded warrior and said, "Because of your failure, you are a disgrace to us." He then raised his knife up in front of the warrior and pushed it deep into his chest.

The dying warrior looked at him and said, "Your time is next." He then closed his eyes.

Dark Eye then told his warriors, "We are going to attack and kill all the ones at Lily's camp. We have been too kind to them for too long. We don't need any of them anymore. I want this man captured alive. I am going to skin him alive and than burn him slowly to watch him suffer. This man is here to challenge me, like others have in the past, but he is going to end up the same way, dead."

The wind started to blow hard and the skies darkened with

heavy clouds. It began to snow very hard. "We will wait until this storm is over. Return here and be ready for a battle."

As I was walking toward Dark Eye, the village people were stepping back away from me. The snow that was falling to the ground was gathering on everyone and everything. But not a single flake had landed on me as I continued toward him. My guardians were trying to show the village people that they were by my side, protecting me, and that I was there to protect and help them. I knew that I had to confront him one on one in order to help protect my people from anymore pain. I suddenly stopped and yelled, "Wait!"

But that did not change what was about to happen. The warrior that I had taken the knife away from approached Dark Eye with another knife and said. "You just killed my brother,"

Dark Eye said, "Yes I did, and I will also kill you," he grabbed the knife from the warrior's hand and stabbed it into his chest twice. The village people knew that the two brothers were very close and it was difficult to witness their deaths in this manner.

In my mind I told them both that I was sorry for physically hurting them but that I would face their killer and try to free their people from him.

"Dark Eye you have caused enough pain and evil here on these people and it is time for you to release your control over them."

Dark Eye smiled and said, "No, it is time to show you that you're a dead man too." He told his men to bring me over to him. I grabbed my shirt and ripped it off my body. Because I felt that when the villager's and warriors saw the eagle, wolf, and warrior on my back, they would realize that I was there to stop what was wrong. Some of them were in awe, because now the sun broke through the dark clouds and the storm stopped. They now thought that the markings on my back and the sun stopping the storm were signs to them all from their ancestors. It was a sign telling them that the dark wrong ways would soon be changed to the right ones.

"No one else needs to be hurt, Dark Eye. This is between you and me. If you think and feel you are whom you are, then face me alone. Or are you afraid?" With those words spoken, he came running toward me. I could feel that there were still some others who were loyal to him and his ways but they were afraid of me. While he was running, he grabbed a war axe and knife. When he reached me, I stepped to the right of him. The war axe touched my side but it had only left a small cut. Dark Eye then leaped toward me with his knife and I moved quickly again to the side. His knife entered a warrior coming up behind me, who also had a knife ready to place in my back. They both fell to the snowy ground and Dark Eye jumped back up to his feet, ready to attack again.

I saw the people from Lily's camp working there way through the others and some stood next to Dark Eye's warriors. When Dark Eye saw Lily, he looked at her with hatred and said, "I should have had you and Fox killed along with your father a long time ago. I guess I am just going to have to do it when I'm done with this one"

"Lily, your brother Fox is alive and you know it. He will return some day soon and he will bring peace and joy back here." A wolf howled. I turned quickly toward his voice. A warrior had shot an arrow at me. I had to stop it because if I did not, it would hit someone else. I caught the arrow as it was about to pass by me. I broke it in half and threw it at Dark Eye.

"You have wasted too many good people and you will soon pay three-fold for all your evil." He jumped toward me again. I grabbed both his wrists to make him drop the axe and knife so that he wouldn't hurt anyone else with them. As Dark Eye tried to break free, I squeezed his wrists with great intensity, which made him drop his weapons. I pushed him to the ground and picked up the knife and axe and handed them to the old warrior from Lily's village. He in turn handed them to another warrior, then another, until the weapons disappeared completely. Now we had to fight hand-to-hand without weapons. I knew that our fighting would end soon. Because I had a quick vision in my head, from my parents, of what was going to happen.

Dark eye began to kick and hit me. He picked up a stone and started to beat me with it. I resisted the urge to fight back. I wanted to give him a false feeling of strength and control over me. He figured that the moment was right.

He wrapped his arms around me from behind and held me tight and said, "I told you that I would kill you. No one can ever win over me."

I knew that I could break his hold on me, but I didn't because I also knew what was to be. While he held me from behind, he ordered his warriors to shoot their arrows at me now. Some of them took aim, but others refused willingly, they placed their bows and arrows on the ground. The ones that were ready to shoot were going to because they were afraid of what would happen to them if they didn't obey Dark Eye.

Some of Lily's people stopped a few of the warriors by saying, "No do not do this. Stop listening to Dark Eye."

Dark Eye yelled out, "Shoot him now or you will have to answer to me later."

With great speed and strength I turned around in his arms and picked him up and turned him toward the arrows that were going to strike me. As the arrows hit his body, a white eagle circled and began to cry out. Then a white wolf appeared and he began to howl along with the eagle circling overhead. They wanted the village people to know that a new way of life was going to start for them.

I released Dark Eye and he dropped to the ground. The evil in Dark Eye's physical body no longer had any control over him because his life was over. His soul would not go into the white light because he allowed his true soul to be absorbed by the evil. If other individual souls, which are controlled by evil, do change their ways to good, they will have the opportunity to walk into the white light. But they will have to pay a price for all the wrong that they have committed.

"If there is anyone here still loyal to Dark Eye and you want to continue this fight, then go ahead. If you wish to leave here, you are free to go, but do not return here for any revenge."

A warrior came forward and asked, "Are you our new village leader?"

"No. I am not the leader of this village. That decision is up to the people who remain here. You all know who deserves to be your leader, or should I say leaders, because they both will do what is right for you. The two of them will always serve, protect, and keep you all safe here. There should be no more need for power or control over anyone because we are all equal and should be treated as such. I know that control, material items, and treasures may make a person feel better than the one standing next to them.

But the truth is they are not because those three items gives an individual a false identity. There are many things that effect life here on Mother Earth and when someone who has been taken over by evil. They can no longer see the true meaning of our existence here. Love for all life, beauty of all things, past, and present, the true inner self of one, and knowing the difference between right and wrong are all lost when one follows the path of evil. This evil causes complete chaos and pain for life and will always be a challenge for us to face. When one stays true to one's self and to the Creator of life, evil will never have the power of control over you, no matter the outcome of the battle."

Lily came to me and asked me if I could stay and help bring her people back together. I told her that I would always help our people, but they must also help themselves. And the only way they can do that is through the truth.

"I will stay for awhile but I will have to leave in time. When I do leave, it will be because my journey here on Mother Earth has much more to do."

## CHAPTER THREE

Fox and the others were about to cross the stream to the village of Buffalo Tear. He saw Red Feather and his warriors standing on the other side of the stream watching them. Fox knew that they were standing there to protect their village from them. Fox told his brother warriors to place their weapons on the ground to show them that they had come to them peacefully. The water was very cold walking into the stream but when they reached the other side they were given warm dry blankets to help take the chill away. Fox and his men thanked the ones who gave them the blankets. A man came forward to Fox and said thank you to them.

"My name is Fox. What are you thanking us for? We have done nothing to deserve a thank you."

"Oh, yes you have, Fox. You and your men have returned to us, Beaver Tooth."

Beaver Tooth then said, "Buffalo Tear, it is good to see you again along with the rest of my people. These men are good warriors. Please treat them well."

"Beaver Tooth, you don't have to say respect and honor because we will always give that to them, for helping you," Buffalo Tear smiled.

"We will have a village meeting so all of our people can hear the true story of great importance."

Fox smiled and said thank you again, "It will be a great honor to speak about this warrior who has opened many eyes and hearts to the truth."

"Come let us get you some food and dry clothing. Then you can rest. In the morning we will all gather to hear of this new warrior."

That evening at the campfire Buffalo Tear spoke about my birth and what he knew about me. Fox, Falcon, White Tail, Crow, Red Hawk, Bobcat, White Owl, Bear Foot, Caribou Ear, and Moose Rib now understood that their brother was a gift. That in the short period of time that they had known me, they were all thankful for what they had learned. They had all promised to follow the path of goodness for themselves and their people. Buffalo Tear's heart was filled with joy, seeing that his people were returning to what needed to be rediscovered in them. And that the young one was fulfilling his destiny for life on Mother Earth.

At the end of the meeting with the village people the next day, Fox and the others spoke of their concern for my safety. They knew of the danger I could be in because of the strong evil that controlled Dark Eye. Fox and the others asked for some supplies and for permission to return to his village to help save me and the other good villagers there.

Buffalo Tear smiled and said, "Yes we will give you all that you need, but there is no need to rush. The Warrior of Truth and your people are safe. I don't know the whole story, but my vision has shown me that there is a new peace in your village. Fox, you and your warriors need to return to your village, to help keep this peace and your people safe. You all are always welcome to come here and please stay in touch with us. If you ever need us for anything, we will be there for you. Remember all that you have learned and be sure to pass it on so that it will never be forgotten. Please tell the Warrior of Truth that we miss him, love him, and hope to be able to physically hold him in our arms again some day."

The days were becoming longer and warmer. The snow was melting and the plants were budding because the sun was higher in the sky, which meant that spring was back. I was glad to see Fox and the others return to their home. Lily was very happy to hug and hold her brother in her arms, and Fox was happy too. The other warriors were also glad to see their families safe and free from Dark Eye's evil ways. We talked together for a few days. When I felt and knew my people had a better understanding of their true selves, I knew that my task at their village was over. I had to move on. When the sun came up in the morning, the village people all gathered and said goodbye to me.

I smiled and said, "This is not a goodbye because as long as you are who you are now, I will always be with you all. With the strength and goodness that you all now have, life here will be wonderful for everyone." As I walked away, I raised my arms above my head and touched my fingers together to make a large circle. This was a sign to them, to show them that we were all connected together as one. Lily knew what the sign meant, so she explained it to her people.

They all yelled out, "Thank you, Warrior of Truth."

After a few days of travel I stood on a sandy shore with a large body of salt water in front of me. It was so beautiful. I sat down on the shore and watched the waves coming to the land. There were many different birds and other wild animals that also came into view. The sun, clouds, and wind, along with the evening moon and stars reminded me of the sacred mountain.

As I thanked Mother Earth for her beauty, my mother and father took form in front of me. We sat together in a circle holding hands for a while and then we began to talk. They told me that they were proud of my accomplishments for our people so far but that I had still other ones yet to do. Father told me that the one emotion to be very cautious of was anger. That this emotion could make you do things that would make you feel sorry for after they were over. When anger takes control over you, you may lose sight of the complete picture. And that could usually mean this; the ones who are innocent are the ones who get hurt. You have to not be blind to its control and its pain. Anger is evil's biggest advantage over good, so remember to always stay in control over it.

Mother then said, "So far, my son, you have shown strength over it but you will face it again. It will come at you stronger, but just remember that we will be with you, to help you defeat its evil ways.

"Mother and Father, I thank you for all that you have done for me so far. I also thank you for your love, which is my strength, for our people. My hope is that what they have been given will remain with them."

"Son, it will remain with them because it was there since the beginning and will be forever. The task is to bring it back to those who have lost it or to those who are hiding from it."


Running Deer and Morning Mist were out of the village collecting plants and herbs which they used to help the sick in their village. They had discovered many different kinds that grew in some areas which were a few days away from their village. Buffalo Tear had helped them both learn how to use the power of Mother Earth to help heal the sick and hurt in their village. Morning Mist was maturing into womanhood; she loved gathering and working with the different plants for their healing power. Flowers were some of her favorites because she felt that their beauty, always gave joy and peace to the hurt. She had planted flowers all through out the village and her tepee was completely encircled by them because they were her specialty.

Running Deer and Red Feather named her at birth Morning Mist because she was born in the early morning in a field of beautiful wild flowers covered in mist. She has always enjoyed the beauty and smell of the different kinds of flowers and now their healing power has given her even more joy.

Running Deer and Morning Mist were gathering plants that they used for medicine when they heard the sound of guns being fired. This sound was new to them because they had never heard guns being shot before. Being curious they went toward the sound instead of away from it. As they got closer they could hear men shouting and the sound of horses running along with more gunfire. They then saw white men on horses battling with each other, coming toward them.

If they remained where they were, the fighting would soon be on them. So they turned to run away, but another group of white men were charging to the battle from their side, and they saw Running Deer and Morning Mist. Four horsemen rode up to them and held them as prisoners. They stayed back while the other white men continued riding forward to the fighting. When the fighting was over, some of the men from the battleground came over to them. The one who was giving orders got down off his horse and walked over to Running Deer.

He started to talk and ask questions. Running Deer and Morning Mist did not know what he was saying because he spoke a different language than they did. When he realized that he couldn't communicate with them, he ordered his men to tie their hands up and place them on a horse together.

They traveled most of the day and made camp just before sun down. Morning Mist and Running Deer were treated all right. They were given food and water. No one was allowed to go near them except a guard. The leader tried a few other times to communicate with them but he was unsuccessful. Running Deer told Morning Mist that she didn't think that these white men were going to hurt them, but because of all the traveling they were getting a long distance away from their village, that their direction of travel had been northeast since their capture, and it was not possible for them to escape yet because they were being closely watched.

One day a lone rider came into the camp, He went right over to the leader and talked for some time. The leader then gave his men orders to break camp and that they needed to get back to their fort because they were under attack there. He told his men to put the two captives on separate horses so that they could travel more quickly. It took two days of straight traveling before smoke could be seen in the distance.

Two guards stayed back with Running Deer and her daughter while the others headed forward at a faster pace to join the fighting going on. The closer they got to the fighting the more worried Running Deer became that they too would also become involved in the fighting. They were able to see the fort and the fighting going on. It looked like the ones inside were winning because of the help that they had just received. The main gate at the fort opened and many men on horses came out and attacked the men outside it.

After a short while the battle seemed to be over. Running Deer and Morning Mist's guards were talking about going to the fort. They decided to go. After a short distance some more gunfire started and the two guards fell off their mounts and Running Deer was also hit. She looked at Morning Mist and told her to ride away. Morning Mist saw that her mother was hurt so she went over to her instead of leaving.

"No, you have to leave, Morning Mist. Try to head for home before they get here. I will only slow you down. So please, daughter, listen to me. Go and warn our people about what we have seen."

"Mother, I love you. I cannot leave you like this."

"I love you too, daughter. But you have to go for our people and me right now. I know it is difficult for you, but it is what has to be done. As long as I walk Mother Earth I will always try to return to you again. So be strong and please leave."

They kissed each other. Running Deer hit Morning Mist's horse on the butt to make him run hard and fast. Some men from the fort rode toward Running Deer and as they approached her, more gunshots were fired at them. A man who was a doctor stayed with her while the others rode off toward the shooters. The doctor helped Running Deer down from her horse and checked out the wound she had in her left shoulder. He told her that it wasn't a serious wound and that he could make it heal soon for her. Running Deer could understand him because he was talking in her native language.

"My name is John and I am a doctor from the fort. I once had a nurse who was a native. She helped me to learn many things about your people and culture. The soldiers told me that they were bringing you and a young one back to the fort to see if they could learn any information about these foreign soldiers. They have been fighting your people and us because they want to take over this country. I need to take you back to the fort so that I can remove the bullet in your shoulder. You can recover from this injury there."

Running Deer asked John, "Can you just let me go so that I can return to my daughter because I'm worried about her safety."

"No I cannot because you have lost way too much blood to be traveling. You need to heal and regain your strength first. I promise you that I will do what I can to see that you are returned to your daughter and your people."

When the fighting was over the soldiers returned to the doctor with some wounded enemy soldiers and a few wounded of their own. John helped Running Deer back up on her horse and they all went back to the fort.

Running Deer was amazed to see the size of the inside of the fort when they rode through the front gate. She had never seen anything in life like it before. It had many wooden buildings with high wooden walls built completely around the entire complex. It had two large wooden gates that opened and closed to allow people to enter and leave. Because of the fighting, some of the buildings were badly burned. There were soldiers and a few natives repairing them.

John asked a soldier for his help. They were going to carry Running Deer to his office so that he could remove the bullet from her. As they started to take her from her horse another soldier who was an officer came over to them and yelled at John.

"John, you take care of my men and the wounded enemy before you do anything to that savage woman."

John yelled back at him and turned around to Running Deer. Two soldiers then grabbed him and they walked away with John toward the wounded soldiers. The officer then ordered another soldier to lock up the Indian woman.

Morning Mist rode her horse fast until she knew that he was becoming very exhausted. She tried to stop his running and when he did, she jumped down off of him. She started walking along side him, still heading in a southwest direction, hoping that she was headed the correct way back to her village. She was feeling very upset because of leaving her wounded mother with people she didn't know. She knew that when she returned to her village, that her father Red Feather, along with some other warriors, would go back to the fort and bring her mother home safe.

After a few days of travel she came to a native village but she wasn't sure what to do. She decided to find a safe place to hide, where she could observe the activity of the village people before she entered it. When she discovered a place, she hadn't been watching them for very long before she recognized someone. He looked like one of the warriors who had come to her village with Beaver Tooth, but she waited to be sure. When she spotted another warrior that she recognized, she knew that it was time to go to them and ask for help.

Red Hawk and Falcon saw Morning Mist walking to them. When she reached them, she stopped walking and spoke to them.

"My name is Morning Mist. I come from Buffalo Tear's village. I remember you two warriors. You were with some others who returned Beaver Tooth and told us about the Warrior of Truth. I have a very bad problem. Can I talk to you about it because I need help quickly?"

"Come with us, Morning Mist. We will take you to Fox and his sister Lily. They will have all the answers you need."

Fox and Lily welcomed Morning Mist to their village. They listened to Morning Mist's story about what had happened. To her and her mother's capture, and then taken to the fort. Lily and Fox were talking together for a little while before they came up with an idea.

"We have learned that by working together, Lily and I can come up with good results for different situations for our people. We will help you; we will send a messenger to Buffalo

Tear, to let him know what has happened. We will not have to wait for very long before we hear from them. Morning Mist, we will do everything possible to bring your mother and you back together again." Lily told Morning Mist that she could stay with her while they waited for her people to respond.

"Thank you, Lily and Fox. I look forward to getting to know the both of you better."

Red Hawk was sent out to Buffalo Tear's village. When he arrived and told the story Red Feather and a few other warriors rode back to Fox and Lily's village. They all sat down together to come up with a plan to rescue Running Deer. Morning Mist wanted to go with them, but Red Feather asked her to stay at the village because he knew she would be safer there.

In the early morning Red Feather, Sparrow Hawk, Running Elk, Crow, White Owl, and Bobcat rode off in the direction of the fort. Before they left Morning Mist told her father and the others to be careful, that the white men had a weapon called guns, and that she had seen many men die because of them.

During the trip to the fort, Red Feather became good friends with the other warriors. They all knew that if there was going to be any fighting, they would stand together for each other until to the end.

After a few days of travel they could see the wooden fortress in the distance. They all sat down together to come up with a plan to get inside it. They saw that the fort was completely in the open on all four sides, and that would make it difficult to approach without being seen first. So the plan was, Red Feather would ride to the front gate with no visible weapons and try to communicate with the soldiers. He figured that they would bring him inside the fort and once he was in there he could try to locate Running Deer. The other warriors would have to wait and be ready for any sign from Red Feather inside the fort. When they received a sign, they were going to make some kind of a distraction to help give Red Feather and Running Deer a chance to escape from inside the fortress.

Red Feather took his knife and made a few cuts on himself to make it like he had been wounded and that he needed their help. He figured that it would be easier to get inside the fort if the soldiers thought that he was no threat to them because of his wounds. As he got onto his horse he told the others to be patient while waiting for the correct time to make their move and to also to be careful.

As he approached the fort, Red Feather could see guards at the top of the wooden walls watching him. When he got closer to the front gate he slumped down lower on the horses back, to make it look like he was badly hurt. The front gate then opened and four men rode out toward him. Red Feather pretended to be very weak. When they got near he saw that one of them was a native. When they reached his horse's side the native soldier asked, "How badly are you hurt? And who are you?"

"My name is Red Feather, and I am only weak from the loss of blood from my wounds."

"Alright. Follow us back inside the fort. Maybe the doctor can help you. But you listen to me, and do what I tell you, or these white men may hurt you even more then you are now."

Once inside the fort Red Feather was surprised to see a group of his people in a small encampment near the back wall.

The native soldier that was with them went to the camp while the other soldiers escorted Red Feather to the doctor's office.

John examined him and he could tell that the wounds were not serious ones. He asked Red Feather, "How did you get these wounds, and where did this happen?"

Red Feather answered, " My woman and daughter have been missing from our village for a few days, so I was out searching for them when I was attacked by some white men. There were too many to fight, so I rode away as quickly as I could and ended up here."

John then said, "You need a few stitches to close up these cuts, but you will heal quickly."

The soldiers who were standing and watching didn't understand what the two of them were talking about, because they didn't understand the native language. John told Red Feather that he could speak freely, that the soldiers were only there to take him to be questioned after he was done. John also told Red Feather that the fort had been under attack by soldiers that were from another country and that they had some native people with them.

"We also have some of your people here that are helping us as well. So when they start asking you questions they will be trying to determine if you are on the enemies side or not."

Red Feather then said, "I am not on their side or your side. All I want is my family back so we can go back to our home together."

John felt that Red Feather was telling the truth about his family. He then asked him their names.

"Running Deer and Morning Mist are their names. And I will do anything to hold them in my arms again."

John looked straight into Red Feathers eyes and said, "Your

woman is here but you daughter is not. I will do all that I can to help bring the two of you back together. But first you will have to go with these soldiers to be questioned by the commander in charge here. I will go to the commander now and tell him that I need to be there when he begins the questioning so that I can help the two of you. The soldiers are going to take you to a room for the time being and lock you in it, until the meeting is arranged."

"John, you are a good man. Your skin should be red instead of white. And thank you for helping and being honest."

John then told Red Feather that he would go to Running Deer and tell her that he was there to bring her home, to stay calm, and go with the soldiers to rest up, and that he would meet him again soon in the Commander's office.

Running Deer was sitting next to a campfire and she was trying to think of a way to escape from the fort. So far she had been treated fairly well, but she wasn't allowed to leave the native encampment. Her shoulder wound had healed and her strength had returned to her, but she wanted to be with her family and her own village.

John saw her sitting by the campfire and he walked over to her and touched her back. "I have some good news for you, Running Deer, but for the time being you need to please remain here until I return. Your man has come for you, but he has to see the commander first and convince him that he is no threat here. I will also be there to help him so that after the meeting, I will bring him to you. I will ask the commander to release the two of you from here, so that the two of you may return to your home."

Running Deer was very excited to hear that Red Feather was near. She thanked John and then said, "I will stay here until you return with him. Please tell him that I love him and that I can't wait to hold him in my arms."

"We will be back here as quickly as we can and it will make me happy to see the two of you together again."

Outside the fort, Red Feather's warriors were waiting for a sign from inside. But instead they heard something happening behind them. Sparrow Hawk told the others that he was going to go and checkout what the noise was. As he was sneaking his way toward the sound, he noticed a huge tree so he climbed up high into the tree. When he saw what was going on, he knew that there was only a little time left for any reaction. He saw many soldiers with big metal guns on wheels and they were surrounding the fort from inside the forest.

Sparrow Hawk climbed out of the tree and hurried back to the others. "We have to go to the fort to warn them because there are many soldiers with big weapons preparing to attack the fort.

Falcon asked, "Do you think one of us can sneak through those surrounding soldiers and try to get some more help."

"No, it is way too late for that because it looks like they are here to destroy this place. Some how we have to try and save Red Feather and Running Deer because this battle will be one of much destruction. Lets go to the fort now."

As they mounted their horses a gun was shot and Crow was hit by a bullet in the back. They all rode off toward the fort with more gunfire being shot at them. As they neared the front gate of the fort, a warrior from inside yelled to them to stop. They had to because the gate stayed closed. Sparrow Hawk then yelled back to him, "There are many soldiers surrounding this fort and they have many large weapons." The front gate was opened up and they were allowed to enter the fort.

In the Commander's office, Red Feather, John, and some other officers were talking when they heard guns being fired. A soldier came in and said that some Indians had just come into the fort and said that the fort was going to be attacked.

Red Feather spoke, "Those warriors are my people. Please do not hurt them because they are here for me and Running Deer." They all left the Commander's office and went to Red Feather's warriors. When Sparrow Hawk saw Red Feather he told them all what he had seen going on. The Commander ordered his men to prepare for a battle. When he heard that the enemy had cannons he knew that they were in big trouble. The Commander then told John to tell Red Feather and his people that he appreciated their help and that they were free to go. When John told them, they decided that they had to stay and fight, that their chance of survival might be better inside the fort then outside of it.

Running Deer saw Red Feather standing next to John. She came running over to him and leaped into Red Feather's arms. Red Feather explained to Running Deer what was about to happen there. John examined Crow, but there was not anything he could do for him because the bullet had hit his lung. When John told Red Feather that Crow was about to die, Red Feather, Sparrow Hawk, Running Elk, White Owl, Bobcat, and Running Deer, circled around Crow to be at his side at his time of death.

The sound of the cannons being fired from outside the fort was then heard. The fort was then hit by the shells. The walls and the building started to fall apart and catch on fire. There were many rounds fired before the cannons stopped. Most of the fort had been destroyed along with many lives lost. The next sound was of soldiers charging the fort from all sides. They were going to attack and kill whomever remained alive.

Red Feather and his warriors, along with some others from the natives from inside the fort were ready to fight. When the enemy soldiers enter the fort, the soldiers who were still alive inside fired their weapons at them. But in a short period of time, the enemy had completely over run the place. Anyone who tried to surrender was not allowed to. The enemy soldiers killed them all. Red Feather and his people knew they needed to fight the enemy soldiers with great courage and strength to the end.

As I was walking threw the forest, I heard a sound. It sounded to me like thunder in the distance but I knew right away that it wasn't thunder. So I headed in the direction of the sound but after a short distance there were many wild animals running away from the noise. I could see and feel the fear that they felt. I felt that whatever was happening now was not a good thing. So I started to run, hoping to get there in time, to help those who needed me.

As I got closer to the sound, I no longer heard the noise that sounded like thunder. I could only hear the sound of many guns being fired. Then at a distance away, I could see many men fighting a battle with great intensity. They were attacking what was left of a wooden fortress. I could tell that the ones inside were going to all die because of all the damage being done there. I, then, felt that there were people inside that place that had been a part of my life. I had to do something quickly to change the outcome of this total destruction.

I asked for help from my parents and guardians and waited for them to give me a sign.

My mother and father came into view and started to speak to me. "There are some things that can't be changed at the time of their happening. But it can be corrected after it is done. Destiny is sometimes a painful experience. Remember that all things that happen at the present time happen for a reason and some are very hard to understand why. You are here to turn some of those reasons into good ones. We are telling you this because this one will be a very difficult one to understand. You must continue your path and be true to your goodness and strength. Always know that we are with you."

Then suddenly in front of me, a few soldiers were riding their horses straight at me at a fast speed. I stood facing them ready to fight when all of a sudden the horses all stopped together. The soldiers who were riding them all fell to the ground hard. The reason why the horses reacted so quickly was because at my side stood my totem, the white wolf. And when the white eagle flew overhead and screamed loudly, the horses all took off running away from the fallen soldiers. Some of the soldiers got back up onto their feet slowly while others stayed on the ground motionless. The ones that were standing pointed their guns at me.

"Okay men, I know that you are following orders that have been given to you by your leader, that you think and feel that you are doing your duty. But at this time you have taken this duty too far. Understand one thing, I will not kill you but I will not give myself to you freely. And if you choose to fight me, there will be pain felt and it will be twice as bad as the pain you have already given to others."

The soldiers all looked at me with wonder because they

had never heard an Indian speak their language so clearly. I was able to understand their language because of the special gift within me. I had used my special gift to communicate with animals and other life forms on Mother Earth before.

One of the soldiers then asked, "Who are you and do you think you can win over all of us?" He then took aim at me with his gun and told the others to shoot on three.

"Wait before you do what your thinking because I can tell you this, death is here."

Their leader yelled "three" and when they fired their guns. Their weapons all blew up in their faces and hands. The barrels of all the guns were plugged up with dirt from Mother Earth when they had fallen from their horses onto the ground. Some of the soldiers were dead, others were wounded badly. No one attempted to stop me when I ran past them toward the fort with the white wolf and eagle at my side.

Morning Mist couldn't believe what she had just witnessed. She had been hiding and watching from a distance the battle at the fort. She couldn't wait at the village like her father had asked her to do. So she decided to come and try and help, but as she came into the area of the fort, she saw too much going on. The enemy soldiers were preparing to attack the fort. She saw her father's warriors being shot at as they were going toward the fort and while they waited to enter inside. When the cannons opened fire on the fort, she saw a lot of damage being done. She knew that many people would die.

Morning Mist asked her ancestors for some help to keep her parents safe. Then what she saw next made her heart fill with sadness, because the enemy soldiers stopped firing the

cannons, and a large group of soldiers was now charging forward, to over run the fort. After a while she saw a group of
soldiers riding toward an Indian warrior who was standing
alone in the open. They were riding their horses so fast toward
him she thought that they were going to trample him to death.
Morning Mist couldn't believe that he was just standing there
waiting for them to come to him, all these men against one of
her own people. But then what happened next, she thought
was a miracle. When she saw the white wolf, and white eagle,
she wanted to run to him. But she couldn't. She felt that the
time was not right yet because the area was way too dangerous. As she watched the warrior move and run, she could tell
by his movements that he was who she knew him to be. They
both had grown up together and they were very close friends.
She also knew that he loved Running Deer and Red Feather
as much as she did.

As I ran toward the fort in the open, I knew that there were
more soldiers out there. One group of soldiers had seen what
happened to the men who had attacked me and they were
amazed. There were two Indian guides with that group of soldiers. They started to explain to them that they had heard of
a warrior who would stand up against bad and injustice. That
he was an individual who would do only the right things for
all lives.

The group leader of the men told the soldiers to attack me
but the two guides yelled out not to. He then looked at the
two natives and said, "All right, you all stay here. I will bring
him back and you three Indians will die together." When he

rode off towards me, one of the native guides started to talk to the soldiers.

"Watch this soldiers, because you may see something that will make you see things a lot clearer. I know this because by watching him and how he reacts when confronted with things that are not right. He will make it right. He will not kill your leader, but your leader may kill himself. And you have already seen this happen to the others who tried to kill this warrior."

I saw a single soldier riding hard towards me with his gun pointed at me, ready to shoot. I stopped running and turned to face him with my totems at my side. As he came nearer, wolf and eagle went toward him which caused his horse to change his direction quickly. He had to drop his gun and grab the horse's mane in order to remain on his horses back.

My totems returned to my side. The soldier made his horse turn back toward me again. I then started to run toward the soldier. We were now both headed straight at each other. The horse and I were about to hit each other. I took a step to his side and grabbed the soldier's leg and I then jumped up onto the horses back, behind the soldier. Then I pushed him off the horse and continued riding to the fort while he rolled around on the ground. The soldier would live but he would have a difficult time moving around with broken arms and legs.

The two natives then told the soldiers, "See, your leader will live. But if all of you had gone with him, some may not have been so fortunate. That warrior could have taken your leaders life more than once. But he chooses to let him live, hoping that he would change his ways in life." One of the soldiers then asked, "Who is this warrior? I have never seen a man move with such speed or have wild animals around him before."

"To our people he is called the Warrior of Truth and it is told that he is a gift not only to us, but also to all things living. His totems and the ancient ones protect him. He has returned what is good to many. Soldiers, I hope you have learned from what you have seen, because you are on your own now. We are going back to our people."

As I rode closer to the fort, I could see that there were many dead bodies all over. When I entered what was left of the fort, and saw all the destruction of life, I wondered how anyone could allow this much death to happen. When I saw Sparrow Hawk, I got off the horse and went over to him. He spoke to me in a very weak voice, "Red Feather and Running Deer are here," Sparrow Hawk then died.

I started to look around for them, and as I was searching, I found more of my people. Crow, Running Elk, White Owl, and Bobcat were all dead too. Then I saw Red Hawk. He was in great pain and barely alive. It was hard to say no to him when he asked me to finish his life. I knew that his death was near and that he was feeling terrible pain.

I held his hand in mine and told him, "Concentrate on my words, and try to forget about your pain. Close your eyes and breath in deeply. Picture yourself at the top of the mountain. The sky is a beautiful blue color with pure white clouds over head. Look at all the scenery Mother Earth has in front of you. Her beauty is all present. Feel the wind on your face, hear her sounds, smell her different scents, and feel her harmony and peace. Look at the beautiful bright white light, Red Hawk. Go to it because your loved ones are waiting for you with open arms. Rest now with complete peace, my brother." He then left this life with a smile on his face.

I felt sadness in my heart because of what I saw in his eyes when I first touched him. I saw Running Deer and Red Feather. Red Hawk had helped them to reach each other because they both had been wounded during the battle. I began searching for the two of them. I hoped that I would be able to see them and touch them before their time was over. After only a few moments I found them and my heart and soul cried for them. I fell to my knees by their sides. I held them both in my arms. They too, were wrapped in each other's arms, lying still on the ground. I had felt a lot of pain before, but this pain was stronger than any other. Then I felt great anger and hatred for those who were responsible for all this destruction of life here. There was suddenly a flash of white light. Red Feather and Running Deer stood with my mother and father beside them.

They all spoke together, "You have to stay strong and not let this anger and hatred you feel take control over you. If it does, you will then be making to many mistakes. The ones who allow anger and hatred to happen to them make things like this happen. Anger and hatred are evil's strongest points and when they take control, you know that it is hard to defeat them."

Running Deer and Red Feather then said, "We know just how special of a gift you are to life. Your parents have explained it to us, so please remain who that you truly are. We are in a wonderful place, but we are very worried about our daughter, Morning Mist. She is going to need a lot of help in order to accept and understand all of this. We love you, Warrior of Truth. Stay the path because you are greatly needed on Mother Earth."

I stood up with a renewed strength and said to them, "I love you too and I will do what is asked of me. Goodness and truth will always be the path that I follow during my journey. I will do my best for you all, to show the honor and respect that I feel for you."

I then heard someone yelling for help but I was not sure where he was. When I heard him calling out for help again, I realized where he was. He was completely buried under debris from a wooden building that had been destroyed. I started removing the debris and I told him that I was there to help him. When I finally reached him, I could see that he needed medical attention right away, in order for his life to be saved.

"My name is John, and I was the doctor here. I thank you for helping me out of this mess." As I began to work on his wounds we started to talk about what had happened. He was very upset over all the loss of life and he wished that he could have somehow prevented it from happening. I told him that Red Feather and Running Deer were very special and I thanked him for trying to help them. When I first touched John with my hands I could see how he had helped Red Feather and Running Deer. I looked up and saw Morning Mist walking toward us. She looked so beautiful and I knew that when she saw her parents that her heart would break.

"John, I will be right back. I have to go to Morning Mist before she sees her mother and father."

"Go to her, my friend. I will be all right. Help her pain because it will be greater than the pain that I feel." As I started to go to her I called out her name and she headed straight to me. When we were face-to-face we looked deep into each other's eyes. It was wonderful to be near her again. I only wished that it wasn't this way, because of what she was about to see. As we hugged each other, I could feel the great concern that she felt for her parents well being. I then held her hands in mine and began to talk to her.

"Morning Mist, your mother and father treated me always like I was their son. I love them deeply and I know that you also love them the same. This will be hard for you, but please believe me because they have told me this for you. They want you to know that they are together and with others they love. They will love you forever and they will always be with you. At some point in time, you will walk together again. They want you to be strong now and continue your journey here with courage."

With tears running down her cheeks she asked to see them. Together we walked over to where they laid on Mother Earth together, in each other's arms. I let her hug them and spend time with them so that she could release the sorrow within her. When I felt that the time was right I went to her side and held her close.

"Morning Mist we will bring them home and take them to the mountain, but please know this. They are there now, that this is only their physical shell that they walked Mother Earth with. We will treat their physical bodies with respect and honor because of the spirit and soul that was within them. Morning Mist hugged me close and tight in her arms and said, "Thank you, Warrior of Truth. I love you. You mean more to me than just my brother."

"I know Morning Mist. You mean more to me than just a sister. I am going to try and find some horses for us. Please go over there to a man whose name is John. He is hurt and needs our help. You can help his body wounds heal because I know you have helped others too. John was a good man to your mother and father; he is also a good individual who tries to do what needs to be done the correct and right way. John is resting over there by that fallen woodpile. I will be right back. We will all leave here together soon."

The soldiers went to their leader who was still lying on the ground. They picked him up, placed him onto a horse's back and rode off toward their main encampment. They went to the medical tent. When they arrived there, the doctor repaired his broken arms and legs. When he became conscious he asked to see the men who had brought him there. When his soldiers came to him, they told him what they had witnessed. And also what the two native guides had said about the warrior who he had faced. He then realized that he was a lucky man to be still alive. He also realized now that he was wrong to think that he could just kill people because of the orders given to him. He remembered his superiors saying that they wanted this new land and to kill everyone who got in the way of things.

But now in his mind he was looking at things differently. He had many questions because of all the experiences he had in this new country. He had seen a lot of death and destruction of his own men, along with others. He now knew that it was all a great waste. He realized that the people in this country were not a threat to his people or his country. That this was just a quest about power and control over a new land and people. Because of all that had now happened they were becoming enemies of the people here. He felt that he was stupid for doing the things that he was ordered to do. He decided that from this day forward he would question any orders that he was given that he felt weren't right. All he wanted to do was to return home and bring his soldiers with him.

When I found five horses I went back to Morning Mist and John. Morning Mist and I took care of the bodies of the warriors who came with Red Feather to find Running Deer. After we were done, we helped John onto a horse to see if he would be strong enough to ride and he was. We then prepared Red Feather and Running Deer's bodies for their return trip back to their home. Together we rode away from the battleground slowly. I hoped that I would never see destruction like it again.

Morning Mist and I talked about our childhood as we were traveling, and all the different experiences we had. Morning Mist then started to ask me many questions about my new experiences, as a young adult. Because she said that she had heard many stores about me and thought they were just unbelievable. She said that she often wondered if they were true before, but not anymore after witnessing the confrontation between the soldiers and me. The doubt that she once had about me was no longer with in her.

Then in the distance I could see many men riding in our direction. "Morning Mist, you have to take your mother and father and go around to that ravine. Follow it until you find a good place to hide and be safe for a while. When you know that no one is trying to find you, leave with caution for home. When you get there, tell Buffalo Tear and our people that I miss them. Give them all a hug for me."

John and I waited for Morning Mist to make it to the ravine before we started to ride toward the men.

As we got closer to them, John said they were his soldiers. The uniforms that the soldiers were wearing and a flag that a soldier was carrying told John that these soldiers were his and not the enemy soldiers, which had attacked the fort. When they saw us riding toward them they stopped and waited for John and I to reach them.

As we were riding closer to them John said, "I will tell them about what happened at the fort. They are going to want to talk to you about it as well.

"John, you don't have to worry about me, because this is just going to be another learning experience for me."

John looked at me and said, "You are quite a man. I will be at your side to help protect and keep you safe with these soldiers." When we stopped in front of the soldiers an officer came to us and asked who we were and why did one rider go in a different direction?

"My name is John. I was the doctor at Fort Ryan. This man next to me saved my life. And as far as I know, I'm the only one left alive from there."

The officer said, "We were going to Fort Ryan. What has happened there?"

"It has been completely destroyed by a foreign nation of soldiers. They had attacked the fort before, but this time they had cannons and many more men than us."

"We were coming to reinforce the fort with extra men, but if it is completely gone, we better return to our fort and inform everyone about what has happened there." He then called out to his sergeant, "You take a couple of men and go after the rider who went the other way."

John then said, "Wait. You don't need to do that because she is returning her dead parents to her people. She and this man here have helped me. Without them, I too would be dead."

"The Commander at our fort is going to want to speak with them because there have been other areas of trouble with their people. We have been told not to trust or believe any of them, that they may say one thing, but then do the opposite."

"This warrior is a man whom I trust and believe. He saved my life. I am here now because he is a good person."

"Sergeant, you leave right now and we will wait here for you to return."

"Wait. Please listen to me first, before you send anyone to do something that is wrong. My people have named me the Warrior of Truth. I will go with you to your commander, or too anyone else, that you would like me to see and speak too. They will believe what they want to, just as you will do as well. I tell you this, you do not need to go after that woman and take away her right of returning her mother and father's bodies to their place of rest. She has done nothing wrong to harm any of you or anyone else. Now if you put yourself in her position, how would you react and feel toward someone interfering with your personal family matters. Because of her parents being killed by white men, she does have a feeling of dislike for you. And if you should interfere now, that dislike could change into much worse. I understand why you have been told to be cautious with us. Because I have seen some of my people with the enemy soldiers that attacked your fort. We can leave right now to talk to your commander because it appears to me that your people and mine have a lot to learn about each other."

The officer then told the sergeant to inform his men that they were going back to their fort because Fort Ryan had been destroyed.

Morning Mist found a good place to hide for a little while. She was sad because she was alone with her parents but she knew that she was doing the right thing by taking them home. After a while she felt that she had waited long enough, that it was now the right time to leave.

A few days had passed before she came to the village of Fox and Lily. Morning Mist told them about what happened at the fort and how the cannons destroyed everything. Fox and Lily were concerned for the safety of their people because they were not sure how they could defend themselves against that type of destruction. They asked Morning Mist if they could go with her, to her village, to speak with Buffalo Tear. They knew that Buffalo Tear would have answers to their questions about how to deal with this growing new danger. Fox and Lily gathered all the people of their village. They held a ceremony for their dead warriors and Morning Mist's parents. When it was over Fox and a few others left with Morning Mist, to escort her to her village. Lily stayed with her village people to keep them calm and safe.

John and I rode our horses next to each other as we traveled back to their fort. We talked about many things along the way. He explained to me about his people's way of life and their beliefs in things. He said that some of his people were farmers and that others lived in towns. That there were also some very big places called cities. He said that the people who lived in the towns and cities had very little knowledge about the native ways of life. The more we talked, the more we both realized that our people's way of living life was totally different. What I was hearing and learning about the white people's way of life gave me a vision. I knew that in the time to come, my people would face some very hard times. I realized that I needed to learn everything that I could about these white people, their thinking and all their ways of living life. I then would return to my people and explain to them what we were going to need to do in order for our survival.

As I talked to some of the soldiers, I also learned a lot from them. Some were willing to speak freely and truthfully. They treated me fairly and with respect, I did also the same in return to them. But there were some others who considered me a person who was way below them. My culture and people could never equal what their standards were. They figured that their advancement of life, and ways of life, had far exceeded our primitive ways. The more that I learned what was to be, I knew that in time my people and our ways were going to struggle to keep our freedom, along with our beliefs, alive.

As we were riding through a canyon I received a quick vision.

I said, "John, tell the leader to stop because there is a trap in front of us, with enemy soldiers waiting to attack."

John rode forward toward the one in charge of the soldiers, he asked them to halt, and not to go anywhere. When he told them what I said, the leader yelled back to me to come to them, so I did.

"How do you know that there is a trap in front of us?"

I knew if I told them how I knew, they would not believe

me. So I had to come up with another way for them to understand that there was danger waiting.

"I can tell because of the different signs I have seen. And if you allow me to, I will prove to you that they are there. You should take your men and go back a ways from here and wait. You can leave a couple of soldiers with me, I will show them where the enemy force is at."

"Lieutenant James, send four men to us and take the rest back a half-mile or so and wait."

"Captain Mike, how long should we wait to hear from you?" The captain looked at me because he wanted me to answer him, so I did.

"We should return within a day. Please make sure that the soldiers you pick to come with us know how to climb on canyon walls."

John then asked, "Can I go along with you?"

My answer was, "John, because your body is still healing, you need to stay with the other soldiers. You will be able to rest up and regain your body strength back."

"If I go with you, I will stay with the horses while the rest of you climb the canyon wall. I will keep the horses under guard so that they will be there for you when you return."

Mike told John that he would have a soldier watch over the horses. That he preferred him to go with the other soldiers, back out of the canyon. And that if we did not return within a day, to just wait for us a little longer, before moving out with the soldiers.

We waited for the four men to come to us. When they arrived we went forward at a slow and quiet pace. After we went a short distance, I could see ahead of us that the canyon walls were taking a sharp right turn. I recognized this place because it was part of the vision I had received. I asked the men to stop and wait for a while. Mike wanted to know what I was doing.

"I'm going to walk over to that corner and climb up only a short ways to see what is around it. You will be able to watch me from here. Don't go any closer to that corner because they could have guards watching for us. That would make a good place for them to be in position to see us, before we could see them."

As I began to make my way to the corner, I walked close to the sidewall to keep myself hidden. Just before the turn in the canyon, I started to climb the rock sidewall. It was a very steep slope at times so I had to pull my body straight up it with only my hands strength. About half way up the side there was a ledge that went around the corner. So I made my way over to it without making any noise. When I reached it, I pulled myself out onto it. I had to lie on my side because there was not enough width on the ledge for my body to lay flat on without part of my body hanging off the edge. I crawled on my side a little farther to be able to see around the corner.

I could now see that the canyon became a lot wider around the corner, that the sidewalls were not as steep. What I was seeing now was also part of my vision, but I saw no one yet. After a short period of time I noticed something that was reflecting the sunlight. It was a long distance from me, but it was on the same side of the canyon that I was on. I waited longer to see if there would be any other signs of the enemy.

I started to see more reflections after a while in different locations. They were definitely there waiting too ambush us.

I then discovered where they had positioned all the sentries. There were two, not far from me, watching the corner of the canyon. The sentries were using something to reflect the sunlight too. They were using the sunlight to communicate with each other. One was across from me and just around the corner at the very top of the canyon wall. The other one was in front of me a little ways and also at the top of the canyon. They were in position to see anyone coming around the corner. And when they did they could inform the others to get ready to attack. With them using the sun for communication I knew that I would have to wait for sunset before I made any movement.

When it became dark, I worked my way back down to the canyon bottom. I moved as quickly and quietly as possible back to where Mike and his soldiers were. I knew if he and his men made a campfire that the enemy would spot them. This would mean that they might come out from hiding and then just attack us. I was running fast without making a sound and I stopped in front of Mike and his men. They all looked at me wondering how I made it to them without any of them even knowing that I was coming. Mike stood up and asked if I had any information about the trap.

"Yes, they are waiting for us and they are well hidden on the canyon walls. There are two sentries at the top of the canyon walls on both sides of the corner. There is no way to get by them without them seeing us coming. In fact, if we do…" I then lowered my voice and said, "We have someone watching us right now. Don't react, just continue to do what you have been and I will take care of this."

Mike smiled and said, "You are something else. How did you know that there was someone out there?"

"I heard him and saw him moving around while I was talking to you."

"I didn't hear him moving. How could you see him in this darkness? Alright Sergeant, get over here because everything is okay. I learned a while ago to always have someone as a back up in case something does happen."

"That is a good idea, Mike. But the next time you do it, make sure he doesn't follow so close. And when he is observing things that are happening he should not be moving around or he will tell them that he is there. We need to get back to your other soldiers and go around this trap. If you decide to confront them, there will be many unnecessary deaths here. We will have to go around this canyon. I understand that it will take longer to get to where you want to go. But you will return to your fort with your men and some new information about your enemy."

## CHAPTER FOUR

Morning Mist was joyful to see her village. Buffalo Tear went right over to her and held her in his arms. "I am so sorry, Morning Mist, for your loss. We all will miss them and their love. We will always honor and respect your parents for all the goodness they have given us. Let's take them to the sacred ground on the mountain."

The village people followed Buffalo Tear and Morning Mist over to the stream. They all walked across it to the mountain's base. Tears were on their cheeks as they walked together to the final resting place of Running Deer and Red Feather. Buffalo Tear spoke a few words about the others who had lost their lives at the battleground. He asked the Creator and the ancestors to please continue to give strength, courage, and wisdom to the Warrior of Truth so that he can continue to follow the needs of his people and all of life.

His last words were, "Thank you, for all that you have given to us here on Mother Earth. Someday we shall all be as one together again."

When they returned to their village, Buffalo Tear hugged Morning Mist in his arms again and told her, "In time to come, Morning Mist, we will need to have a very important talk. But for now you need to rest and regain your strength. When you are feeling better you will be given a sign to come and see me. I will help you to understand what you will need to do. Please know that I love you like your parents do."

As we rode back to Mike's other soldiers, he began to ask me many questions about who I was. He was asking these questions because of what he had already witnessed and also heard from others about me. I could feel that Mike's inner self was good, but he had made some bad and wrong mistakes. He felt guilty and sorry for what he had done and he was having a hard time living with it.

I told Mike, "You needed to follow your correct path in life. Do not close your eyes to what is right or wrong. What was done wrong in the past can be done wrong again if it is not corrected now. And if some how you can make the wrong be right, then do it, to correct it."

He started to tell me what it was that he could not deal with, that he had done. I touched his shoulder and told him to wait to tell me the story when we could speak in private. When I touched him, I saw what had happened. It was very difficult to handle and it caused a lot of pain in my mind. I felt that I had to give myself some time to accept what had happened and not judge him for it. I hoped that maybe he would make up for that terrible act, and live the rest of his life doing what is right, never doing wrong again.

As we rode along without talking any longer, the story

started to reshow itself to me. It all began when he was a young officer. He was told by his commander to go to this Indian village to find their chief. And they were to bring the chief back to the fort to be questioned about some incident. As they were going to the village they found a white family that had been killed. They had been mutilated and scalped. They were all enraged with great anger so when they reached the village they attacked it. They ended up killing men, women, and children and then they set the village on fire.

The white family was innocent and Mike discovered later, that the village that they had destroyed was also innocent too. He learned that the ones responsible for the death of the white family were natives from a different village.

We stopped to set up camp for the night. Mike came over to me and asked if he could tell his story now. John was with me and he stood up to leave but Mike asked him to stay. "I think I need to let others know this story, instead of just the ones higher up in command."

I looked at Mike and said, "Some of the ones in command of you will not ever tell the truth because it will hurt their ruler-ship."

Mike lowered his head and sat down on the ground. John and in I sat down with him.

"Mike, before you tell the story I want you to know that I all ready know it."

"How do you know it?"

"I know it because of who I am, and I also know that you are carrying a hard burden inside you. First I want you to understand this; you reacted to the emotion called evil anger. This anger had complete control over you, along with the others that you were with at the time. It had so much control over you all, that you were all blind to the true fact of what had really happened. Nothing mattered but revenge, which is also pure evil. The fact is, this negative and evil energy will always exist and look for its opportunity to completely control an individual. You and some of your men carry this pain and sorrow because of the good in you. Your true inner self knew that it was the wrong thing to have done. But at the time you were too weak and blind to see that. And that is why you are in pain now. The ones who don't feel this and who actually enjoyed killing and destroying that village are true evil and will always continue to be. You and the ones who know the wrong of this have rediscovered your true selves. You want to correct the mistake and never allow it to happen again. That is a good thing to do. The important lesson learned is this, now you and the others have to be always aware of that evil. That it exists and not to ever be blinded to its presence again. You will have to face it again, and when you do, follow your true inner self to defeat it this time with your goodness."

Mike looked at me and said, "In the short time I have known you, you have shown and taught me so much."

John also smiled and said, "I too have learned things, along with my life being saved."

"The two of you remain strong and good and always follow the right path. You might take a step in the wrong direction, but always correct it, my friends."

Morning Mist was standing by the stream and she was thinking about going to her parent's resting place. Fox walked up to her and started talking. Fox asked her if she would return to his village with him. He told her how he felt about her.

He promised that he would take good care of her. She was honored to have him speak to her so truthfully. But during the whole conversation, she saw in her mind another face. She knew that Fox loved her, and that she did feel love for him as well. But that the love that she felt for Fox was different than the love she felt for the one who she truly wished for. She had never told him what her true feelings were because of who she knew him to be. She kept her feelings to herself so that he could do what he was suppose to, without having to worry about her.

When Fox finished talking about how he would like to spend the rest of his life with her Morning Mist hugged him and thanked him for his respect, honor, and love. With tears in her eyes she hugged and kissed him. She told him that she loved him too and that she always would, but that there was another who she loved and that she was waiting for him. Fox understood and wished her well. He then left to go home.

Morning Mist was upset because she realized that this was the sign that Buffalo Tear spoke about, so she ran over to his hut.

Buffalo Tear was waiting for her with open arms, "Please come inside, Morning Mist, because we have a lot to talk about." Once inside they sat down together and Buffalo Tear started to talk. "Years ago I was told of this moment so I will start by explaining this from the beginning. The young one came to me when he was just a boy and he explained to me how he felt about you. At that time you both were very young and had much to learn about life. We are all here for a purpose and I know that it is very difficult to understand it at times. You are here now because you need to understand why you didn't go with the one who loved you, standing next to you.

Instead you choose the one who was only in your mind at the time. The reason for this is because your love for him, and his love for you, is like no other; it is called true connected love.

"No matter the distance between the two of you, your love is always there. Please believe that there will be a day that the two of you will be together. From that day forward your lives together are going to be filled with happiness. The two of you shall be as one forever more. Some of us never learn why or what we are to do here on Mother Earth. But this man has known since the day of his birth, because he has been chosen to show us who we were meant to be from the beginning. The only problem is this; there is way too much wrong here on Mother Earth for one like him to correct it all. He has done all that has been asked of him, and in his helping, he has given back what has been lost and hidden to others here. You, Morning Mist, are a very important part of his life. He is also that in yours. I understand that it is hard right now because the two of you have not had much time together, but you will soon. Believe me because I have seen the two of you or should I say three of you, together."

They both smiled with joy. Morning Mist no longer felt confused because she now understood her true feelings.

"Buffalo Tear, I love you, and I thank you for helping me, and also all of our people love you too."

It had taken many days of travel before we reached Mike's fort. This fort was very large with a lot of soldiers inside the compound. There was also a small native village located near the back wall of the fort. Mike said that the natives were scouts for them, that they and their families were good people.

That the commander in charge of the fort was called Colonel Luken. Mike said he would go and talk to the colonel first. He wanted John and me to stay where we were because he knew that the colonel would want to meet us. Mike walked over to the commander's office and went inside. John and I sat down on a bench with Mike's sergeant.

We hadn't been sitting for very long when two men came toward us. They were not soldiers. The closer the two of them came to us, the more I could feel their hatred. The sergeant told them to stop and when they didn't he stood up in front of them. The one closest to him drew his gun and smashed the sergeant in the head with it, knocking him to the ground.

John then asked them, "What do you think your doing? You just hurt a soldier."

"Who is this Indian scum? Where did you catch him?"

"He is not a captive, but a friend of mine and also to the man you just hurt.

"Well, he is not my friend and I will show you that he isn't."

He went to kick me hard, but I caught his foot and stood up straight. I lifted his foot above my head. He dropped to the ground on his back, hitting his head hard onto the ground. The other man then leaped at me, all I did was take a step to the side as he flew by me and hit the bench. I went to check out the sergeant and helped him to his feet.

The sergeant looked at the two men and said, "I am going to have you both arrested and put behind bars. You have made a big mistake, but if you think you haven't had enough yet then continue your fight. If you draw a weapon you will be the one who dies."

Some other soldiers and native scouts were coming over to see what was going on.

The two men stood up and the one said, "Two of us against all of you?"

I then said, "No. You two are against me because no one else needs to be hurt by you. I understand the reason you both feel hatred toward me. If you think that you need to hurt and destroy me, or my people, to make your hatred go away, then use it on me. But remember this, the ones who have caused this hatred in you have made you the same as them. You may have been innocent before the pain you carry now. But the ones you hurt now could be innocent too, which means that you have now caused the same pain to others who should not have to feel it. All that you are doing is strengthening the evil that started it all. I will not destroy your life, but I do hope to take away that evil that has control over you."

The two men came and stood in front of me very close. The one on my right side who hit the bench had some doubt about what he was doing now. The other was still looking for revenge because of the death of his friends. He swung his arm around to punch me in the face, but I moved so fast that his punch missed me and hit his friend instead. Now he was really mad so he again tried to punch me a few times. All I did was move quickly so that his punches never made contact. He was getting more frustrated which only meant that he was losing more control over himself. His friend no longer wanted to fight so I made my way over to him to speak. The other one took a break to catch his breath because he had wasted a lot of energy.

I stood next to the man and looked straight into his eyes,

"If you are a good friend to this man, you need to help him to rediscover himself before it is too late."

He then said, "I do understand what you are saying to us."

He took a step in front of me and started yelling at his friend to stop fighting. But his friend walked over and pushed him out of his way so that he could face me head on. He then pulled a knife out and tried to put it into my body. I grabbed both his arms and threw him to the ground. He rolled on the ground away from me and then sat up. He threw his knife at me but I moved out of its way. I then realized it could hit someone. I reached out and caught it just as the point of the knife's blade touched his friend's chest. The sergeant ordered his men to place him under arrest for attempted murder. An old Indian warrior walked over to me and asked me if I would come to their camp. I told him that I would, but that I first had to meet the commander of this fort. John was checking out the man's chest to see how bad he was hurt. I went over to them to make sure that he was all right.

"He is one lucky man to have had you here because no one else could have stopped that knife."

I looked at him and said, "You are trying to do what is right and your friend has a ways to go yet before he reaches that point. You need to help him, but you must continue to follow your true self because you are doing what is right now. And that is the only way you can help bring him away from the evil that has control over him."

The colonel, Mike, and a few other officers were standing outside his office on the porch watching the whole incident. Mike began waving his arms and calling out to John and me to come over to them. Mike introduced us to his commander and the other officers. Colonel Luken told John that he was sorry to hear about the fort and the people there. They talked for a while about what had happen and who was responsible for all that destruction.

Then the colonel turned to me and said, "I have been told a lot of interesting things about you. Now what I've seen with my own eyes tells me that you are a very special individual."

"I don't consider myself as a special individual; I am not any different than any other human being. I will die when it is my time. I bleed when I am injured and I feel all the different emotions that we all have. But I will never let negative or bad ones control any part of me. It is important for all who walk Mother Earth to discover their true selves, and to follow their correct path here. We must honor our Creator and the ancient ones who have walked Mother Earth before us. I know that bad and evil will always exist and that there will always be a struggle to keep it in check. It is always good to do what you feel and know is the right thing to do against it. If you're not sure, then you need to look deep into your true self because the answers to any questions that you have about doing what is right is there. Your people and mine have much to learn about each other in order for us to live together in peace. Your ways of life, and ours, are different just as all other cultures are. The one thing that is the same for all others, and us, is a simple word. That word is love. Love for all life is the only savior for us."

A man dressed in black clothing stepped over to me and said, "I am a teacher of God and speak words of good and truth like his son, Jesus. Have you been educated in our religion and bible?"

"No, I have not been. Your beliefs are yours and mine belong to me. We know that all life is a gift from the Creator.

He may be called a different name; honored, and respected, in different ways because of people's different beliefs. But he is who he is, just as we are who we are. And when the time is right we will be as one together. As it was in the beginning, the circle never ends until all that he has created here, is no longer here. And that will only happen because of us doing what is wrong and not right."

When Colonel Luken called me by my name, the man dressed in black said no more.

"Warrior of Truth, you are a man of honesty and you are welcome here and free to do anything that you need to do. If you do need anything please let Mike, John, and me know what it is so we can help you. I hope to talk to you some more at your convenience. I'm glad to have met you."

John and I left the colonel's office and walked over to the old warrior's camp area. A young little girl came running over toward us just wanting to say hello. The old warrior was walking slowly behind her, coming to us too. I kneeled down at her side and touched her hand. She was not born here at the fort, but she lived here now because her village and most of her people were taken from her. She would now be raised in a different environment where she would be learning new things. Which in the future could be helpful for her and her people, but she needed to remain who she was now in order for her to do that, for them. At her age we are all full of good love and innocence, but as we grow older the bad and evil become a challenge we all must face.

The old man told John and I that she was his granddaughter. That her village had been destroyed and her people were killed by an enemy village. That he and his granddaughter along with a few others escaped and came to this fort for help.

After a while some of the warriors decided to go to other villages and ask them for help to take revenge on the ones who had destroyed their home. They did find others who had trouble with this village too so they went there to take care of the problem. And when they arrived at the enemy village they watched over it before they attacked. They discovered that there was a big change in the place. So instead of attacking it they went in to see if they were correct about it being changed. They were told about a warrior who had faced the evil there and defeated it alone.

I then said, "No, a warrior did not defeat the evil there. The people of that village defeated that evil, with the goodness of their true selves."

"My warriors were told that chief Dark Eye no longer exists because of the Warrior of Truth. And I hoped to meet him someday before my own death, to thank him for his deed."

"Please listen to me old one. Chief Dark Eye was defeated but by his own people. Because they finally realized how much bad he had done, and that they had done, by listening to him. So they wanted to correct it and make things right. The arrows from the bows that killed Dark Eye came from ones who were still under his evil control. But once he was defeated by his own evil, many were set free from it."

"Warrior of Truth, is there evil here and is that why you have come here?"

"Evil is always close and waiting to find someone weak enough so it can take control of them. My main reason for being here is to learn more about the white man's way of living. When I have learned, all that is needed to be learned, and I feel that the time is right, I will return to our people and try to make them understand the white man's ways. If we can respect each other and accept each other's beliefs we will live in peace together."

The old one looked at me with a lot of doubt in his eyes and said, "During my time here with these whites I have seen many things that our people will not accept. They have a lot of rules that make no sense and there is no way that we will accept them. I just think that our people and our way of life is in great danger because we cannot be like them."

"I understand what you are saying. I promise you that I will do all that I can for our people and also the white people. The both of us need to find a way to compromise our ways, in order for us to live together."

John touched my shoulder and said, "Tomorrow we will talk to the colonel and see if we can go to the big city. You will see and learn all that you need to there, my friend."

The old Indian warrior then said, "This man, John, is a good friend and he can tell you a lot about his people."

"I don't think John is just a friend because he is my brother. He has already explained a lot to me about his people and their ways of life. I have also told him about ours. John has told me about his government, their laws, beliefs, money, and their views about us. But I need to physically see it and be involved in their lifestyle, for me to be able to explain it correctly to our people. I know that there are many good people like John who do what is right, when it needs to be done right. Our only hope is that the good in his people and our people will out way the bad in both."

I then called the old one by his name, which made him smile because no one had told me his name. "Gray Wolf, you are a good guide here. Continue to keep our people safe and happy. We will meet again some time."

In the morning Mike, John, and I went to Colonel Luken's office. We sat and talked for a long while about the many different ways of our people. He said that it was a good idea to go to the big city to get a better insight of things. Colonel Luken told Mike and John not to leave my side and to keep me safe. He also asked Mike to bring a couple of soldiers with us for added protection. I felt that this learning experience was going to be a very interesting one. I had already learned much about the whites and their ways. The colonel, Mike, and John spoke freely and honestly to me because I spoke the same to them. Our ways of life were really different and we knew that in order for peace among our people, a change would be necessary for each of us.

We continued to talk the entire day and our knowledge and friendship for each other became much stronger. I told them that I would tell my people about how good that the three of them were to me. And that they would always be welcome to come to me and my people. That they would be treated with respect for all their help and goodness they have given.

The three of us, along with some of Mike's soldiers, left the fort at sunrise. It took us four days to arrive at the outskirts of the city. There were so many large buildings and a lot of small ones as well. Some were businesses and others were homes. In the stores one could buy food, clothing, tools to work with, and guns. They would use money, and yellow stone, which was called gold, to get what they wanted. These two things were very important items in the white people's lives. It was easy to see that money and gold was something that they all wanted and needed. And that it was a big control factor in their lives.

I then saw a bank and this was supposed to be the place where the people would put their money and gold, to keep it secure. The next building that I saw was called a church, and it was very beautiful inside. But I did find it hard to understand why a man called Jesus was on display on a cross. I knew it was a part of their religion and their beliefs. But I felt that this man should be remembered, honored, and respected, in a more beautiful way, instead of a painful one. It would be wonderful to see Jesus praying to our Creator, and his, instead of his sacrifice.

A man who was a part of the church and the religion came over to me and we began to talk for some time. He was a good man and he was one who would follow his correct path in life with teaching what was right. We both learned a lot while talking together. But I still did not agree with how they remembered this man by his way of death. I understood that Jesus's sacrifice was for life. And that there have been others on Mother Earth who have also made sacrifices too. There will also be some other individuals in our future, willing to give themselves freely, to help life to continue on Mother Earth. A man doing and being who he was should be respected and honored in a much better way.

The next place I saw was a business called a saloon and this place did not make much sense to me. Men would drink alcohol and this stuff would change their state of mind completely. It would make them be who they were not. A good man could become bad, and a bad man could become even worse with alcohol. I witnessed fighting, gunfights, and a bank robbery because of men drinking.

One day Mike and John took me to a courthouse where a trial was going on to show me how their justice system worked. I learned that some were correct punishments for the individual, but others were not. I understand that there are rules and laws that one most follow and when they are not, then a price is paid. But what I witnessed during some of the trials, I did not agree with. Because sometimes bad won over good and that was not right. And it was hard to understand why the people there would allow this to happen. The main reason for this was because it was written as a law and their decision about the case had to follow the written law. I felt that if the written law was wrong, why was it not changed to make it right. And why didn't the man they called the judge, who was in charge of the proceeding, do something to make it right, instead of wrong.

My next lesson was another one that meant that there would be big trouble to come. I already knew that money was a problem because of what the white people wanted from it. The ones who had a lot of money had power and control over the ones with less of it. I learned that banks helped people but they also hurt them. The ones with more money in the bank system, again, controlled the ones with less. They would loan money to people to buy land and other things. But when they couldn't pay back the loan at the correct time, the bank would take their purchase away from them. And all the money that was given to the bank before they couldn't pay the loan now also belonged to the bank. So someone else would gain the profits, and the ones who had tried to make the purchase, were now left with nothing. I had a hard time understanding the fact that the land that was always free to us, now belonged to the white's, because of money. And if this were true, the land that my people lived on would be taken from us because we had no money to pay for it.

I felt that I had learned and seen enough, that it was time for me to go back home to my people. I knew now that my people were going to be in great trouble in the future because we could not completely adapt to these white people and their ways. My only hope was that my people and our culture would not be completely lost. The power and control of the white people would overwhelm us for sure. My people and our ways have a special meaning with Mother Earth. It is going to be difficult for us to accept the white people's ways of living. They are way too wasteful to Mother Earth and also too full of greed for her.

Mike and John and some others did prove to me that there are some white people that do what is right and good. They understand that we are equal and that there is no need to have control or power over anyone, but themselves. They have seen wrong and evil and know they have become warriors against it. I also know that there are others like them out there, but there are not enough. Because of our different ways, my people and I will always be considered beneath them. That their ideas and standards about life are so different than ours, they may never be viewed as the same.

Mike and John knew I was ready to leave the city. John asked me if I would like to see one more place that was called a school. I told him yes, but after the visit to the school, I would like to head back to my village. Mike told John and me that he was going to send a message to Colonial Luken, to ask for permission to go with me. When Mike left to send the message, John also asked if he could return with me, as well.

"The two of you are welcome to join me. It will be a good learning experience for you both. I have seen and learned a lot about your ways of living and you both will also learn and see ours."

John and I went to the schoolhouse. It was a very interesting place. The children there were being educated on many interesting facts. They learned how to read and how to do math, science, and things about the past that they called history. These young ones were taught good things from their teacher that were very important, along with doing correct things, the right way. I could see that there advancement started at a young age, which allowed them to be much smarter in the technical field when they became older. If these children could stay who they are at this time and not change when they grow up, our different ways could have a good chance of joining together in friendship.

Mike found us as we were leaving the school and he told us that the colonel needed him to return to the fort with his men. I looked into Mike's eyes and told him, "You are a good man. Remain who you are now with strength. And if a time should come and you have any doubt about a decision or an act, I feel you will do what is right because of the goodness within you."

He then touched my shoulder and said, "Warrior of Truth, this world could sure use more like you. Thank you for making me more aware of myself. You have a safe trip home."

Mike then shook John's hand and also thanked him for being a good friend.

John smiled and said, "Yes brother, you have a safe trip back to the fort too." We stood together laughing and talking as brothers a little longer.

There were people watching and wondering why these two

whites were being so good to an Indian, who they consider a savage.

A group of men started to walk toward us.

One of them asked, "What is this savage doing here in our city, and why are the two of you acting nice to him?"

Mike and John both spoke, "This man is not a savage, but a man of honesty and he is our brother."

A few of the men had bottles of liquor in their hands, which meant that they had been drinking.

John then told them, "If you guys are looking to start something, go start it somewhere else."

A man threw a liquor bottle at John, but I caught it and dropped it on the ground. Mike told them that they should leave and go back to the bar, while they could still walk.

One of the drinkers answered him, "There are only three of you and twelve of us. And we are going too kick your butts so you can't walk."

I didn't want John or Mike to get hurt, so I started to talk, "All right, you guys are here because you feel that I'm an insult to you and your precious city. You also don't like the way Mike and John treat me because you think and feel they are an embarrassment too you and your people. By the way, the stuff that you are drinking gives you all a false identity of who you really are. So if you think that by beating on us will make you feel better, you are thinking wrong. Leave my two brothers alone because I know I am the reason you are acting like you are. I will only defend myself against your anger and hatred. I will not kill anyone, but some of you may get hurt during the fight. And in the morning when you wake up in discomfort, know that you have caused it to yourselves. You guys could just turn around, go back to your saloon and wake up with only a headache."

Mike and John laughed and some others in the crowd of people who were watching did too. But it wasn't funny to a few of the men who wanted to fight so they began to advance toward us. A couple of men jumped at John and Mike. The ones who rushed at me were surprised when I moved quickly by them and pushed the men away from John and Mike. They were about to attack again when a gun was shot. The city's sheriff and some deputies were walking toward us. The sheriff was the one who fired the gun because he wanted the fighting to stop and it did.

The sheriff asked, "All right, what is this fighting all about?"

Mike told them that we were from the fort and we were about to leave the city, but that this group of drunks wanted to have a fight because of me. The sheriff told us that we should leave now, that he would keep the drunks locked up for awhile so that they would not follow us. Before we walked away I went over to the sheriff and thanked him for doing the right thing.

We left the city and after a day of traveling together, John and I needed to go in a different direction than Mike and his soldiers. They were headed back to their fort and John and I were going to Buffalo Tear's village, my home. Mike started to say goodbye, but I told him not to say the word. I told him that I didn't like to hear that word because to some it means they will never meet again.

"We will meet another time and place, my brother. Stay strong and continue being the man you are."

John and I rode our horses at a slow and easy pace because

we had a long ways to go before we would reach my people's village. I felt happy inside knowing that I would soon be with Buffalo Tear, Morning Mist, and also with the others that I loved. I missed the sacred mountain and was looking forward to physically feel and seeing its special beauty in person.

During my daily meditations I would always spend time on the mountain. It had always been apart of my true self, and me, and the sacred mountain always will be. The mountain spirits and I are connected together, not only for this lifetime, but forever.

I told John all about Buffalo Tear and the others in my village who were special individuals to me. John told me that he looked forward to meeting everyone and he hoped that he would be accepted. I smiled at him and told him not to worry about being accepted because he already has been. That when my people see what I see in him and know him for who he truly is, he will be one in our family and given a new name. I told him that his white man's name, John, will remain. That his new native name would be one of honor and respect always, from my people.

John looked at me and was about to tell me his feeling toward me, but I spoke to him first, "John, I know what you are going to say to me and I want you to understand something first about me. We have known each other for only a short period of time. I know that you wished that we had met sooner in life. You know that I am different from anyone you have known and that I will always stand for goodness. One gift that our Creator has given to me is the sight and feelings of knowing things. I know people for who they are, good or bad. My purpose here is to always try and make good win over bad, and to make right, what is wrong. You don't have to thank me for anything because you already have by following your true self, which is good. You will learn a lot about my people's way of life. There will be a time when you will return to your people and face a difficult challenge. You will try to make your leaders understand our ways, and stop them from doing wrong things against us. You will need all your strength and wisdom to carry you through this task. I do know how it will be and I want you to know this. Because of you and your love for us we will always be remembered. I thank you now, my brother."

"Are you telling me thanks now because you won't be around later?"

I did not answer his question so he stopped his horse. He then jumped off his horse and walked over to me with his eyes watery, "I wish I could give you something special, Warrior of Truth, to show you that I will follow your truth."

With a smile I said, "There is something, John. And with this we will always be as one on Mother Earth."

I removed my knife from its sheath and cut the palm of my hand, I then handed the knife to John. "If you cut the palm of your hand, be careful not to cut it too deeply, and then you grip mine. Our blood will flow together as one and we will always be united here on Mother Earth and where ever else we are. You and I are now blood brothers, we shall always be that."

When Mike and his soldiers reached the fort, Colonel Luken asked him to join him in his office as soon as possible. They talked first about all that had happened at the city. The colonel then told Mike why he needed him to return to the fort.

It was because he had received orders from higher officials to send out troops to gather information on Indian village locations. They then talked about the problems that these orders were going to cause on the natives and their people. They both knew that they had to come up with a way of following these orders in a peaceful way, for both sides. They knew that they would do it the right way, but there biggest concern was how the other commanders at other locations would handle the orders. They also knew that some would not do it in a peaceful way or the right way. And they knew that it would cause a great loss on both sides.

They were interrupted by two soldiers and a native scout. We have discovered enemy troops moving in large number with cannons toward our fort. They are definitely up to something that could bring a lot of trouble here. Colonel Luken told Mike to ready the soldiers at the fort and send a messenger to the city to also warn them.

"We need to be on full alert and ready for any attack from them right now. Also get some more scouts out there to keep us informed of their location and actions. If these men are the same ones who destroyed Fort Ryan, we have to defeat them here, to stop their advancement any farther.

# CHAPTER FIVE

I could see the sacred mountain in the distance and I looked forward to being there. "John, the mountain is only two days away. We will soon be home."

As we rode forward I suddenly felt we were being watched. I told John that we needed to get off our horses and walk because we were being watched by some others. After a short distance I received another feeling and it was good.

"John, it is alright because the ones who are checking us out are my people."

I stopped and raised my arms above my head. I was waving for them to come to us. Beaver Tooth couldn't tell who I was at first, but when he saw me waving at them, he knew who I was because he had seen me do the waving before. After he told his warriors who I was, they all came running toward John and me, so I ran toward them. The joy and happiness to see my people was a wonderful feeling to feel.

When Beaver Tooth and I came together we held each other in a bear hug and then the others joined in. I told them that John was a man to trust and that he was also a part of us, to please treat him with respect. When we walked back to John he showed his respect for them by kneeling down and raising his arms up like I did. Together we all laughed and then we grabbed his arms, and hands, and lifted him back up onto his feet, to stand together with us.

That evening we sat around the campfire talking about the entire happening that occurred, which had brought John to us. Morning Mist had already told the village people about a white man whose heart was good. Beaver Tooth said that Buffalo Tear had also told our people that a day would come when a white man would live with us. That he would be one who would stand at our side and protect our ways of life.

When I heard the words that Buffalo Tear spoke, it made me wonder if he to knew what our people were going to face soon. I couldn't wait to be with him, to see if he had been given anything hopeful for our people's future.

We were ready for sleep so we all laid down on our backs. The stars in the evening sky became active by falling to Mother Earth. There was a full moon, with beautiful bright white stars in the sky, forming different shapes of the animals here on Mother Earth. This was a special gift of sight given to us from our Creator. I knew that this was a sign and that it was important. I also knew that Buffalo Tear was also seeing the same happening, that he to also knew it was a sign of great importance. We were both being told that we would soon be united, and that we would both need to be strong for our people because there was going to be a lot of change coming in our people's way of living their lives. And that we all had to always remember and believe in our ways of life, since our beginning. When I closed my eyes, my heart felt heavy with sorrow because of what I knew would be, and so was Buffalo Tear's.

After a few days we came to our village and standing there waiting was a man with others happy to see my return home. I jumped down off my horse filled with happiness and love for them all. It was wonderful to be with them all and to hold them in my arms. When Morning Mist and I held each other, I had a vision that made me happy and also worried. But for now the worried feeling would be put aside for the stronger feeling, which was love.

The love that we felt for each other was strong and I knew that I would have to talk to her later about the other worried feelings. For the rest of the day we all celebrated being together again as family. When the sun lowered behind the sacred mountain the wild animals and the ancient spirits there also celebrated my return. The animals did with their voices and the spirits with their beauty and color. I thanked them for their protection and help and for showing me their respect on my return home. I asked Buffalo Tear to join me in the morning for a visit to the sacred mountain. We both knew that we had much to discuss. And we both hoped that we could come up with answers to what we knew was going to happen.

At sunrise Buffalo Tear and I met at the mountain stream, we were excited to be going to the sacred mountain together. John, Beaver Tooth, Morning Mist, and a few other villagers were also there. Buffalo Tear told them that we would return in a couple of days and not to worry about us. He asked Beaver Tooth to stay with John and to take him around to meet the entire village.

Morning Mist hugged Buffalo Tear and came over to me. When I held her in my arms I told her that when we returned from the mountain, we needed to talk, I then kissed her cheek. Buffalo Tear and I walked across the stream, turned around and waved to them all. As we started to walk to the sacred mountain we began to talk to each other.

"You have learned much and you have also been a very good teacher, my son. I want you to know that I am proud and thankful for all that you have accomplished."

I looked at Buffalo Tear and said, "I too am proud, and thankful, along with the ancient ones, for all the good that you have done. We both have had a special journey here on Mother Earth and we both have still much to do."

We both smiled and stopped walking because in front of us, looking straight at us, stood our totems. A large white buffalo with a white wolf, and white eagle, were together waiting for us to come to them.

Buffalo Tear then said, "The power of three is a strength that no evil can ever defeat. We may not be able to physically remain together, but for as long as we are, our people here are safe from any wrong."

We walked over to our totems. We both touched them and thanked them for their protection. As we continued to the mountaintop our totems followed us. It was almost evening when we reached the place that we felt we needed to be at, in order for us to join together as one, to help our people. This place was special because it was here that Buffalo Tear, White Cloud, and the Warrior of Peace, also joined together. I knew that we would soon be seeing them along with some others as well so that they could help Buffalo Tear and me to understand what was needing to be done for our people's survival.

The stars were very bright and so was the moon, which made the night a beautiful sight to see. Buffalo Tear and I sat facing each other, touching our hands together. Words did not need to be spoken because we were in a much higher state of communication. Buffalo Tear was able to see and feel all of everything that I had experienced with our people and the whites. I was also able to see and feel what he had been through as well. He knew all about what I had learned about the white people and what I knew was going to happen to our people.

I saw that he had always wanted our people to follow the path of righteousness and goodness and that I was a gift from the ancient ones, to help him make our people stay the right path in life. As we became deeper into each other, there was all of sudden a beating of drums and our people singing.

Buffalo Tear and I stood up on our feet and turned too see our people. They were beating on drums, playing flutes, singing and dancing together. We stood there listening and watching them. We knew that what we were seeing was before our time on Mother Earth. They were our ancestors showing us a dance that had been forgotten. The dance was giving respect to the sun, moon, stars, sky, and all of life on Mother Earth. It also honored the Creator for giving us earth, wind, water, fire, because if one did not exist then neither would life itself.

As we were watching, an ancient warrior came to us and said, "The two of you learn this and please teach it to our people. Once they have learned this, it will always stay with them for as long as Mother Earth exists. It will help them to remember who they are, and who they were, in the beginning. You both know that change is something that will always be. Some is good; some is bad, and very hard to accept. The bad you do not have to ever accept, because you know the good, and what is supposed to be right. You two are always the light of goodness for our people. You will keep our people remembered."

I then asked him, "Are you telling me that what I know about our people's future is truly going to happen?"

When he lowered his head, Buffalo Tear and I looked at each other. He didn't have to answer the question with words because his body language told us the answer. They all started to fade away slowly and when they were completely gone, Buffalo Tear and I sat back down with sadness in our hearts. We knew the fate of our people and what our purpose was to be. Together we sat in silence thinking about how we were going to be able to explain this fate to the ones we loved. We sat for a long time, before we were then given another sign. We heard the sound of buffalo running, a wolf howling, and an eagle screaming.

The sun was beginning to come up and the sky was a bright red in the east. Then a white light came from the heavens and some forms began to take shape in front of us. My mother, White Cloud, and father, Warrior of Peace, were the first ones to appear. Then Red Feather and Running Deer also came into view and behind them there were a few others. My parents reached out and touched Buffalo Tear and me. They thanked us both for helping our people.

"Mother, Father, and the rest of you, how can Buffalo Tear and I stop what we know is going to happen to our kind? I understand that change is always in life, but this change for our people has too much destruction for our ways and us. Do we lose everything that we have been given by our Creator?"

They all said no together and my Father started to talk. He said, "Our Creator's gifts for life is truth, goodness, and love, and it will never be lost. No matter how much evil destroys, it can never take away what is in everyone. Love, truth, and goodness are in all of life. Some may not see it or follow it, and others don't feel it because it is hidden within them. But it is there and all that lives life on Mother Earth have it because nothing exists without it. So know that what ever happens, as long as life is here on Mother Earth, there will be truth, love and goodness. With the two of you, along with some others here on Mother Earth, our people and their ways will never be forgotten. And yes, you are right. There will always be changes involved in life. But the two of you, and also the some others, who are strong with this righteousness, give hope to those who have been lost of it. We understand the many challenges you have to face here because we once walked Mother Earth too. Please know, that others like you in the time to come will continue helping life see and feel what our Creator wants for us to follow."

"Father, I understand what you are saying, but I only wish that when there is change, there would not be so much suffering and pain."

My mother touched me and said, "Son some change is all about control and power, which brings things at times that are not good."

Buffalo Tear then asked, "Is that type of change the reason for us being here? To give hope and goodness back to those who have had it taken away? It seems that all my life here I have tried to fight wrong, and help those who were in great need. But what I have learned from this is that no matter how much good you do, the bad is always there waiting. I think that as long as we walk Mother Earth, there will always be someone, groups of individuals, wanting power and control over another. And that means to me that there will always be conflict amongst us. We have good and bad, right and wrong, respect and disrespect, belief and disbeliefs, truth and lies, love and hatred, two of everything. I know that our purpose is to do all that is good, but can we ever completely abolish that which is wrong? Or will wrong some day abolish good?"

There was silence for a while among us. But then Red Feather and Running Deer came over to me to talk. "We know your love for Morning Mist and we know her love for you. The two of you together will bring much joy to us if you both would become as one. Fear not the future because it is important that your time together happens now."

White Cloud and Warrior of Peace came and stood next to Red Feather and Running Deer. They held each other's hands. Then the others moved over with them and formed a circle around Buffalo Tear and me. They all held hands together and began chanting to us. They all started to glow a very bright white color. Buffalo Tear and I could see and feel the true love, respect, and honor that they felt for us.

As they were slowly fading away to leave, my Mother and Father looked at the both of us and answered Buffalo Tear's questions without speaking a word.

"You both are right about the existence of good and bad on Mother Earth. But if bad does become so strong that it does abolish good then all life on Mother Earth will be no more."

I thanked them all as they left, and told them that I loved them and that Buffalo Tear and I would pass their love on to our people.

The evening sky was beautiful and bright with stars falling in the heavens. Then there were bright colors flashing through the sky. Red, blue, green, yellow, and white lit up the heavens with flowing beauty. Buffalo Tear and I knew that Morning

Mist and the others in our village were also seeing this beautiful gift that had been given to us.

Morning Mist and the others were standing along side the stream looking up at the top of the mountain. They could see that the top of the mountain looked like it was engulfed in a bright white light. The light grew dim the sky became alive with falling stars and color. It was then that she saw her parents smiling down at her and she was very happy to see them. As she waved to them and said she loved them, she heard a voice say, "Follow your heart and soul." She knew what it meant because in her mind was the man that she loved, and wanted to spend the rest of her life with.

Buffalo Tear and I knew that we needed to remain strong, in order for us to continue the path that had been given to us. We stood together listening to the different sounds of Mother Earth. The wild animals all started calling each other and the birds were all singing. All the wild life was responding to the rising of the morning sun and a new day.

I said, "Buffalo Tear, did you receive the complete answer to your questions about good and bad or right and wrong?"

"No I did not, but I could tell that you did before they left and that you would share that with me."

"Yes I will, but I know that you will feel much pain from this truth. Our destiny is what it is and we must do what we know we are too do, which is right. There will still be time for us and our people to live our lives as we do, and we must be there for them. What we give of ourselves to them will always be there for them, because it always has been from the beginning. Allow only the good to come through you when you see and feel all the bad that is to come, when you have your answers to your questions."

I then held Buffalo Tear in my arms because I knew that if I didn't he would fall to the ground in great pain from what he was about to see and feel. His body did go limp and he cried like a child for a long time before he was able to recover from the pain. As I felt his strength return we sat down together and we both closed our eyes and fell into a deep sleep. We both needed to rest to regain our physical strength, as well as our inner strength.

While I slept my dreams were very intense. I saw many years into the future and what it would bring to Mother Earth and its people. There was much I didn't understand because of all the advancement and new technology that now existed in our world. I also had seen that people in that time would still be having a difficult time trying to live together. I saw many changes in Mother Earth as well because the people no longer showed her respect. They had destroyed a lot of her beauty and poisoned her badly.

I woke up to the sound of Buffalo Tear playing a wooden flute. The sound of it had gathered the wild animals on the mountain around us. There were all types of birds, deer, bear, wolves, mountain lions, rabbits, raccoons, and elk, along with their babies. When he saw that I was awake he stopped playing the flute and the wild ones walked away without any confrontations among them.

"Your playing of the flute is very delightful, Buffalo Tear. Have our people heard it because it is very soothing and healing to the soul?"

He smiled and said, "Not yet, but they will when we return. Our people will also be shown our ancestor's dance of respect for Mother Earth. When I woke up this flute was in my hand. It was a gift. So I played it for the ones who gave it to me. When we do return home what we now know will have to remain with us or our people will panic. It is our duty to prepare them for the changes to come, so that our kind will not be completely destroyed and lost. The two of us, and a few others, will help our people understand their destiny. And the ones who do understand and accept it, will be the ones who save our people, our beliefs, and our ways."

We both knew and understood all the pain, suffering, and destruction to come to our people. But because of who we are, along with some others, we will continue to walk Mother Earth in our way until the end. When we leave Mother Earth there will be others who will take up where we have left off, and continue to do and be the same as we are now.

"When we return home, Buffalo Tear, would you please be a protector and guardian to a very special individual to me."

"I already am, and I always will be to her, just as I am with you. I have known for a long time that the two of you would be together someday. I know how you both feel toward each other. The love that you have for our people, and for her, is the same love that I feel too. That is the reason for us to be, and do, who we are, and it will always be."

"Yes, you are right, Buffalo Tear. Let's go home and follow our paths. I thank you for being in my life."

# CHAPTER SIX

Mike and a few soldiers were slowly moving toward the enemy camp. They were hoping to capture someone with information about what the enemy's plans were. They split up into small groups of three men each and spread out around the camp perimeter, looking for officers. After a short period of time Mike realized that something was happening because there were soldiers running to the left side of the camp. He then heard guns being fired; he knew that some of his men had been discovered and that they were in trouble.

The shooting didn't last very long. Then he and the two men with him saw four of his soldier's bodies being dragged through the camp. They saw two of his soldiers wounded walking with guards around them. Mike watched the enemy soldiers place his soldiers in a tent with guards outside it. It wasn't long before an officer and another soldier entered the tent that his men were in. Mike wanted to save his men, but he knew that the odds were against him. Mike also knew that the officer inside the tent was going to question his soldiers.

And that they would try to get all the information they could from them in many painful ways.

Mike and his two soldiers saw an enemy soldier walking straight toward them. He motioned to his soldiers to lay flat on the ground and he also did the same thing. But he was ready to take down the soldier quickly if he came close enough to him. He could hear him getting closer with each step he took. When he placed his foot down next to his side, Mike tripped him and hit the back of his head to knock him out. Mike's two men came over to him. Mike told them to cover the soldier's mouth and to tie him up so that he couldn't escape. Mike took off his uniform and exchanged his clothing with the captives. He told his men to take the captive back to the horses and wait for awhile. And if he didn't return they were to go back to the fort with the captive. His soldiers followed his orders and moved slowly and quietly back toward the horses.

Mike stood up and worked his way over to the tent where his soldiers were. As he got closer he could hear them talking inside the tent. The guards didn't pay any attention to him because they figured he was also a guard who was just walking around the camp perimeter. Mike waved at the guards to get them to look in his direction. He then began to point at the outer perimeter trying to get them to think that he saw something. And that he needed them to come over to help him look for what he saw. The guards turned away from the tent and walked over to the area he had pointed at and began searching.

Mike than moved over to the tent and went inside it with his gun in hand. When the two enemy soldiers inside saw him they went to reach for their guns. But Mike's men recognized him and knocked the two enemy soldiers down. Mike told them not to move or say anything or they would be hurt. He untied his men's hands and told them to change uniforms with the two enemy soldiers. The officers then told Mike that he and his men should just give up now. And if they didn't give up, they would all be killed as soon as they left the tent.

"Well, if we are killed, then you will be because we are going to leave here together. I am here to save my soldiers and others from your kind. This is not your homeland. The pain and destruction you have caused here has got to stop. My hope is that it will end with no more destruction or pain for either of our people. If you come with me peacefully maybe we can find a way to stop the fighting between us. And if we do, I promise that I will do all that I can to see that you and your men are sent back home."

The officer said, "I'm not the one who is in charge here. I only follow the orders that are given to me. So if you think you can stop what is going to happen by taking me, you're wrong."

"Okay, I understand what you are telling me so all I want from you is a 'yes' or 'no'. Are your commanders planning to attack the fort and town?" The other soldier told the officer to say nothing.

Mike smiled and then said to the soldier, "Thanks for answering my question for him.

"Now I have something to say and make sure your commanders hear it. We know that you are planning to attack us. But what you don't know is that it will be your last attack here on our land. And that when the fighting is over, none of you will return home and most of you will die. The ones who live will spend the rest of their days in a prison. And those days won't be very many because of who you are and what you have done here to us. We know all about your other attacks on our forts and people. So we are now ready for you and if you want proof here it is.

"Men tie these two up so they can't move and place something in their mouths so they can't be heard. We will let you live for now, but not when we see you again. Make sure that your higher up officers know what I have told you. So that maybe they will decide to retreat and go home, or just stay here and die. Lets get out of here, men, because we have things to do."     Mike looked outside the tent to see if it was safe to leave. It wasn't safe because he saw that the guards were returning. Now he had to come up with a new idea in order for him and his men to get out. He went over to the enemy officer and told him that there were guards outside and that he didn't want to hurt them.

"If you give them orders and send them away then we can leave without anyone getting hurt or dying. It will be your choice and I hope that it will be the right one."

Mike removed the officer's gag so that he could speak to his guards.

The officer said, "You have to untie my hands so that I don't look like a prisoner."

"No, I will only let them see your face while you give them their orders." Mike opened the tent flap so the officer's head could be seen.

The officer called to the guards and when they came over to him, he told them. "Go and get a doctor because he is needed. I want both of you to go together to get the doctor. Keep your eyes open for anything unusual because our prisoners have told us that we are being watched by them." When the guards turned to go, Mike closed the flap on the tent.

"I know that we don't have much time and that when they return with the doctor, you'll be out looking for us. And I think that we both know that if we do meet again it won't be a good time."

When the officer was bound back up and gagged Mike and his men left the tent and slipped away into the darkness of the night. They reached his other two soldiers and the captive just before sun up. They quickly mounted their horses and headed back to the fort. When they arrived at the fort, Mike went straight to Colonel Luken's office and told him what had happened.

They both questioned the captive guard and learned that the enemy could be stopped. They were going to set the soldier free with a message for his commander. The message basically said the same things that Mike had already told the other two in the tent. It said that they had two days to retreat and go back to where they were from. And if they didn't then they would be attacked and eliminated from this land. For those who survived, there lives would be ones filled with misery and pain just like they had caused here. And that they would never return back to their homeland.

When the enemy commander received the message, he read it. The other officers under his command also read it. They all decided that it was time for them to leave this land because they were still able to do it. The main reason for this decision was because they had been in this country long enough to know that they could not take it over. There was way too much land and too many people to conquer completely. So they figured if they did stay and continue the fighting, the letter was right, they would not ever be going home.

The order was given to prepare the men and equipment

to return to the sea and too board their ships for home. They knew that there quest here to own, and rule this land, was over.

Mike and the colonel were glad to hear the news from their scouts that the enemy troops were headed away. Colonel Luken asked a few of the scouts to keep track of their movement to make sure that they would leave the country.

Buffalo Tear and I walked down the mountain slowly talking about our lives and what we needed to do. When we reached the stream we both stood still and took in the beauty of our village now. Because we knew that there would be a time when what we were seeing now would be much different.

Our people started gathering on the other side of the stream to welcome us home. It was wonderful to see them all because they were always happy and joyful to see us return from the sacred mountain. They had always been delighted to learn what Buffalo Tear was given on the sacred mountain.

But this time we would have to teach and inform them of what we knew very slowly. Because if we didn't the disappointment and hurt would be way too much for them to handle. We both knew that we could not just come right out and tell them all about what was going to happen. It would be way too hard for them to accept it, and they all would panic. Buffalo Tear and I would have to explain everything very slowly to them, so that they would be able to understand and accept their destiny, one step at a time.

Beaver Tooth and John came over to us along with Morning Mist. Our people all started chanting a song to us. Buffalo Tear smiled and said, "They will soon learn a new chant."

Morning Mist wrapped her arms around me. She hugged me tightly. I kissed her and she kissed me. I also looked deep into her eyes and asked her if she would allow me to be her man. Our people, Buffalo Tear, and John, all began yelling and jumping with joy.

Morning Mist then kissed me, and then said, "Yes, I love you, Warrior of Truth, and I always have. You have just given my heart all that I would ever need here on Mother Earth and my life is your life."

"Yes, my love, our lives are connected together as one."

Together we joined our people in singing and dancing. It lasted all day and well into the night. Buffalo Tear came over to us and blessed us together as one. When the ceremony was over we continued the singing and dancing for awhile longer. We all stopped and sat down in a large circle on the ground.

We all were very tired so we laid down and fell asleep on the ground under the moon and bright starlit sky.

When the sun came up Morning Mist and I went to Buffalo Tear and told him that we were going to do a little traveling around. And not to worry about us, that we would be returning shortly. Buffalo Tear hugged both of us, and told us to be careful and safe. He knew that I was going to start to teach and explain to her, about what the future had in store for us.

For the first couple of days we spent time enjoying the gifts of Mother Earth; her waterfalls, valleys of flowers, hot springs, animals, sunrises, sunsets, all of her beauty that she has given to us. We had many long conversations about the past and present occurrences in our lives. Morning Mist understood and accepted well the reason why things were the way that they were. Morning Mist understood that our journey here on Mother Earth had a special purpose which we have to follow it and also accept. The hardest things for her to understand were why evil and wrong would sometimes win over what was good and right.

I explained to her, "That, yes, it might win for a while, but at some point in time, it may lose completely. And when the good and right returns, it will be stronger to those who have lost it. The ones who remain good and true to what is right, will become even stronger when that evil is gone. If there is ever a time when bad becomes stronger than good, then wrong does overpower goodness, and life on Mother Earth will be no more. That kind of evil could even destroy Mother Earth first, and then us."

Morning Mist then said to me, "I know that you are special. Can you please tell me all that you know?"

"Yes, my love, I can. But you need to be much stronger than what you are right now. Because if you knew the complete truth about things that are to be, it would be too over powering for you just yet. Physically and mentally you would be in too much pain to handle what is going to be. When I know that the time is right I will tell you all that I know to keep you safe. I will gradually teach you, but for now let's enjoy what we have in front of us; our love for each other and our people, along with Mother Earth, and our Creator."

As we continued our traveling around, I told her about the white men and how they lived. I told her about the city of whites that Mike had taken me to and how their ways of living there, was so much different than ours. She asked me if our people would ever be able to live their lifestyle or be able to adapt to it.

I told her, "In time, we would have to adapt to their ways, so that our ways, would not be forgotten. Some of our people are going to have to accept this change, in order for them to survive. When we return to the village, I would like you to come with me to a special spot on the sacred mountain. You will experience the strength and beauty of our ancestors and Mother Earth, and that will also strengthen your inner self to a much stronger level. The mountain and all the spirits there are a gift to us from our Creator, to help us see and understand all of life. It has been from the beginning and will be until the end, our place of internal knowledge."

All of a sudden I could hear the sound of guns being shot. Then Morning Mist and I could see a huge dust cloud forming in the distance. The dust cloud was from a herd of buffalo, running away from the ones who were shooting at them. Morning Mist became afraid because it looked like they were coming toward us. As the buffalo got closer, we could see the large herd running right toward us.

"Morning Mist, lets mount our horses and be ready to move if we need to. But for now, let's continue to watch and see what this is all about."

As they approached, a large buffalo who was leading the running herd saw us, and he changed their direction of travel. When all the buffalo ran by us with great power and speed, I could feel their fear. At the back of the herd, there were some babies following. There was one that was very special. He was the last one in the herd and he was also a sign for me. He was pure white and as he ran by, he looked directly at Morning Mist and me. Morning Mist said that he was beautiful and she hoped that he would not be hurt. Now I had the feeling that we had to go back to our village. Being white and small, his message to me was that things were going to be starting soon. I needed to remain close to my village and people for now, to keep them protected. Morning Mist and I turned our horses toward home and rode off.

Back at the village, Beaver Tooth and John were becoming close friends. John was learning what it was like to live as a native. He saw that nothing was wasted and that everything was shared. If someone needed something for survival it was given to them. Everyone was treated with respect in the village and whenever there were any problems. Buffalo Tear would always have the right answers to solve them. John asked many questions so that he would have a good understanding about the Indian ways of life. He had learned that the beliefs in the Creator, and the spirit world, were very strong among all the village people.

Buffalo Tear explained to John the meaning of the sacred mountain, and why it was such a special place on Mother Earth. He told John that with each step taken on the sacred mountain one gains great knowledge. And as you step closer to the top, the soul of ones self becomes pure and stronger, because of what is learned.

Buffalo Tear told John, "The Warrior of Truth was born on the sacred mountain. He was to give life here strength, in all that is good and right. Everyone who walks Mother Earth has a purpose, and he knows this, and he also teaches others what their purpose is. Some may not follow the correct path because of all the outside interference that they are blind of. When bad and evil can control the weak, then conflict, destruction, and pain will happen and you have seen this. All the people here on Mother Earth must always be aware of the evil that exists among us. Because the more of us it controls, the bigger the conflicts, destruction, and pain becomes."

John then asked a question that Buffalo Tear had heard before. "Do you know if people can ever totally take down wrong and evil?"

"There are some who can and always will. But there will always be some who are too weak and they will live their lives in evil. There are always two ways of seeing and feeling things. There is up and down, in and out, hot and cold, yes and no, light and darkness, love and hate, happiness and sadness, laughter and crying, water and fire, today and tomorrow. For every action, there is a reaction. Life is full of many changes, which we have to face, with courage and strength. Those who do it with goodness and righteousness help those who have lost their way or who are unsure which path to follow. And those who are pure evil will not ever change. So the answer to your question is, evil will never be totally defeated until the life as we know it to be, is no more."

John reached out and touched Buffalo Tear and said to him, "Thank you for awaking me, and allowing me to see with open eyes, the truth that is right in front of me. Because of you and the Warrior of Truth I feel that I now know. For the rest of my days on Mother Earth, I will do and follow all that I can for what is good and right always. I have learned so much and I feel that my inner soul will always respect and love all that I have been given. Thank you."

Morning Mist and I rode into our village. It made us happy to be back home. Our people were also happy to see us and they were saying that they had a gift for us. Morning Mist asked them what the gift was, but our people wouldn't tell us what it was. They all smiled with joy instead. When Buffalo Tear came over to us I could see in his eyes what the gift was and I was filled with joy.

But before anyone said anything I whispered to Buffalo Tear, "Did you ask for permission for this gift?"

He smiled and said, "Yes, of course. I did and I had been given the permission to do it."

"Okay, my people, please take us to our gift from you. I thank you all for your love, and your gift of love to us." Morning Mist was going to ask them again what the gift was, but I held her hand and told her to wait to see it.

As we walked toward it, John asked Buffalo Tear, "How did the Warrior of Truth know what the gift was?"

Buffalo Tear's answer was, "The Warrior of Truth is an individual who is a very special gift from our Creator, to all life here on Mother Earth. He is called the Warrior of Truth because that is who he is. He knows all that is true, and he gives it all in return to all life here on Mother Earth. We need him and all that he stands for now. But I think there will be a time when he will be needed even much more than at the present time."

In front of Morning Mist and me was a beautiful hut. It was built on a small ridge across the stream on the sacred mountain. I could tell that its location would allow us to be able to see the entire village, and our people. Morning Mist turned to me with tears of joy in her eyes, and then she turned and hugged Buffalo Tear. Morning Mist and I thanked our people for their wonderful gift of love to us. Together we walked across the stream and when we reached the other side we turned and waved to our loved ones. As we made our way to our home I thanked Mother Earth, the wild life, and the sacred mountain spirits, for allowing us to live here on this special ground. When we reached our new home we looked down to see our village below us. Our people were all jumping and cheering with joy when they saw us hug and kiss each other at our home.

As we were waving to them, the animals on the mountain also welcomed us by showing themselves to us. The first one was an eagle flying above us and screaming 'hello.' A wolf was next with its mate and three little ones. The five of them began to howl together. They also were saying 'hello.' Then there was a bear, mountain lion, deer, rabbits, and other wild ones. They, too, were all saying welcome here and 'hello' as well. Morning Mist was very excited to see that we were accepted on the sacred mountain by all the ones that also lived there. I told her that we would always have visitors here, and not to be ever be afraid because they were all our guardians here. We sat and listened to all the wild life and watched the sun set and the moon and stars rise in the sky. We knew that this day was one that would always be remembered in our souls.

# CHAPTER SEVEN

Fox and Lily were sitting with some of the elders of their village. They were discussing a problem that had happened when a few warriors were out hunting. The warriors discovered a herd of buffalo and they were going to try and hunt them for some food for the village. As they were preparing to get closer to them, guns were fired at the buffalo from another ridge. Many of the buffalo were killed before they could escape the gunfire. The warriors waited to see what the shooters were going to do next. They watched the white hunters go to the dead buffalo and take their hides from their bodies.

They saw the hunters take only a small amount of buffalo meat and they just left all the rest of it to waste away. When the white hunters left the area, the warriors went to the down buffalo and gather all the meat that they could carry, so they could bring it back to their village. There was still a lot of meat left behind and wasted because the white hunters had killed way too many of the buffalos, the warriors could not carry all of it.

They realized if the whites continued this kind of action, that there would be a great problem finding food for the village people. There were also reports from other village warriors that the white men had been looking for yellow stone in the rivers and mountain areas. They learned that the whites called the yellow stone 'gold' and it was suppose to be of great value to them. They had also heard that in some of the areas where the gold was found. A lot of building things and land destruction was happening because of the large increase in white people being there. This meant that sooner or later there would be trouble because of what was being taken by the whites from them. There were also other reports of the whites killing other wildlife besides buffalo. Deer, bear, beaver, fox, wolves, elk, mountain lion, and many other animals were being killed for their hides. This was a serious problem because the whites were taking away what was needed for their survival.

Fox and Lily were trying to keep everyone from panicking because they knew that if they didn't, there would be a war soon. A young warrior came running into the meeting yelling that a group of white soldiers were coming toward the village. Fox told everyone to remain calm, but to be ready for any attack. He then ran out toward the approaching soldiers to stop them. He was able to meet up with them, just outside the village grounds. He asked to speak to whomever was in charge of them. One of the soldiers asked him who he was "My name is Fox and I would like to know, what is your reason for coming to my village?"

"We are here to ask you some questions, and to inform you of what is expected of you and your village. We will camp right here and send a scout to you when it is time for the negotiations to start. And when you do return, bring with you the ones who make the decisions for your village with you."

The soldier then ordered his men to set up camp and to place guards around it. As Fox turned to walk, the soldier told Fox to keep his people away from their camp. Fox told the soldier to also make sure he kept his men away from his village.

His words made the soldier mad, so he said, "We do and go were ever we want too."

Fox wanted to respond, but he figured that it would just make him madder, so he just started walking back to his village. When he entered his village, some of his warriors were waiting. He told them to place guards around the entire village and to also stay away from the soldier's camp. He then went to Lily and told her what was happening. They both felt that something not good was about to happen and that they needed to stay alert. They both hoped that they were wrong about how they felt. But they knew that shortly, they would know for sure, what would be happening.

John and Buffalo Tear were walking through the village when they saw a young child lying on the ground crying. They went right over to him to see what was wrong. John saw that the child's leg was hurt. Buffalo Tear picked him up and they went to the child's tepee. John told Buffalo Tear and the boy's mother that his leg was broken. And that for the leg to heal correctly, the bone needed to be placed back together. The only way to do it right was to operate on it, but he did not have the correct items needed for the operation with him. Buffalo Tear asked him what was needed to do the operation for the child. John explained the tools and medication for this task would be difficult to find here. But Buffalo Tear told him that they had all the medicine and tools that he needed, and that he would help him with the procedure.

"They are going to be different items than what you are use to using, but they will do what you wish them to do for you."

So they gathered everything that was needed and sanitized all the tools. The child was given a medication that made him sleep. It also took away any of the pain that he was feeling. When it was time, John operated on the child's leg and repaired the badly broken bone.

After a few days the child started to feel much better. John did not want him to move out of his bed yet because he needed the leg to heal more. So he spent time with him to make sure that he rested and remained still. He would tell the young child many different stories, that he remembered his mother telling him when he was a little child.

He told the boy that he would soon be as he was before his injury, but that he needed to go slow and easy until he was totally healed. The village people all thanked John for helping the child's leg to heal. They were all very happy to see him take his first steps again. The child became stronger with each day and it wasn't long before he was able to run with his friends once again.

One day Buffalo Tear and John were standing next to the stream talking. John always enjoyed his conversations with Buffalo Tear, along with the others in the village too. He felt that this was the greatest time, and part of his life, so far on Mother Earth. The child came over to Buffalo Tear and John. He asked them to come with him to his tepee. Buffalo Tear told John to follow the child, because he knew what the child was going to do. A few village people were waiting there for them. The child went inside the tepee and came out with a special gift for John.

He handed a necklace to John that he had made, he then said, "Thank you for helping me and healing me," to John. The village people all said thanks for being such a good man to them, and for helping the child to walk again.

Buffalo Tear then told John, "That necklace shows everyone that you are a part of us and that you always will be. The crystal stones and herbs on this necklace represents Mother Earth's healing power. The feathers, bear claw, and wolf hair, represents wild animals and their strength of goodness. This necklace and your goodness will help keep you strong and protected during conflicts with wrong and evil.

John then spoke to them all with tears in his eyes, "In all my life I have never felt or seen what I have experienced here. I am so honored to be able to be a part of your life here. I promise you all that I will always be at your side when you need me. I wish that all those who live on Mother Earth could be as you all are here. The words; hate, war, and wrong would be words of no existence. Thank you all for everything that you have given to me. I love you."

A few days had passed before a scout from the soldiers camp came into the village of Fox and Lily. He told them that the talks were to start as soon as they would come to the tent that was between the village and their encampment. Fox told the scout that at sun raise they would come to the tent without any weapons for safety purposes. He also asked that the soldiers inside the tent would also do the same.

Just before sunrise Fox and Lily, along with a few elders,

walked to where they could see the tent. They waited to see what soldiers would come to the tent before they moved any closer to it. As it became lighter out, they saw a group of soldiers moving toward the tent. They all stopped when they saw that the natives were watching and waiting for them. One of the soldiers turned to the others and said something to them. He then turned and started walking towards the tent with only five other soldiers. The other soldiers stayed where they were. Fox and Lily with four elders started to walk toward the tent as well. They all stopped at the tents entrance to introduce themselves.

Lily spoke first, "I know that we are here today for a reason. And my only hope is that when this is over, no one will be hurt."

A soldier then said to her, "No one will be hurt if you do what you're told to do." Fox knew that soldier was the same one who he had confronted a few days ago before when the soldiers first arrived. The soldier was about to speak again, but another soldier told him to shut up, and return to the others that were left behind.

"My name is Mike and I am sorry about that soldier's attitude and disrespect. Let's go inside the tent and do our communicating. I will be honest with you and I hope that you will be the same with me."

They all entered the tent and sat down at a long table that had chairs around it. Mike spoke respectfully to Fox and Lily and also to the others. He thanked them for coming peacefully and said that he hoped that when the talks were over, that the peace would still remain.

"I know that this land is very important to you and your people and your way of life. But because of our way of life and the needs that my people think they must have, is why I'm here. Many of my people have ventured into your area, and they have changed things already in your ways of living. The leaders of our people feel and think that they need to be able to control you and your people. And by doing this, they think that they are protecting all those who are coming onto your land.

"I understand that all native tribes have been here longer than any white people. There has already been many conflicts between us in different parts of the country. Your people and mine have both been killed because of foolish reasons. Do you think that we can somehow find a way to live together in peace?"

Fox and Lily looked at each other because they understood what Mike was talking about. Fox then said, "You sound like you have a kind heart Mike, and I wish that I could answer that question. But to be honest with you, we think that because of our ways of life, and yours, we will have a lot of problems. With each passing day our food source is being taken from us and also wasted. Animals have been killed, then skinned, and left to rot away. When we take the life of an animal we do it with respect. And we also use all of it in many ways. For food, clothing, and tools for our survival. They are not wasted in any way. We give our wildlife respect and honor for there sacrifice. We have also been told that some whites are looking for yellow stone, that you call gold. This rock called gold is something that your people believe is of great value to them? Some of our people have already died because of this gold and also the hides of animals. With all these things happening I don't think that your people, and ours, will ever find complete peace among us."

One of the soldiers with Mike started to speak, "We have had reports from other areas that your people have attacked farmers and wagons that were traveling to new homes. The ones you killed had nothing to do with taking anything from you and your ways of life."

Fox then said, "I understand what you are saying because that has happened to both of us. Innocent ones for some reason are always the ones that pay the price of something not right. There are a lot of things that are being done that is not right. Both of our people have to be careful of what we are told because sometimes it may not be the truth. If we are not there to actually see what happened, then how do we respond to it? When a story is told, how do we know if it is true or a lie? How do we trust and believe a story if we are not present to witness it happening ourselves?"

Mike looked into Fox's eyes and said, "I understand what you are saying and I agree that there has to be some kind of proof of happenings in order to believe it. I learned a while ago from a man who I believe opened my heart and soul to the facts of many things. I have learned from him to follow my inner self and to do what is right and good. Before I had meant him, I had made many mistakes, and did not correct them. But now if a mistake is made, it is corrected, and that path will always be the right one for me. I am here to try and help both our people. I think that you are as well. I tell you this, my higher up officials are going to try and make agreements with your people, on where they are going to want you be living. They are saying that they are willing to try and trade material items, along with food, and different places for you to live. They do want to try and keep peace between us. The only problem is that we both have a major situation to deal with.

Some will do it right and others will not, and that will cause a lot of trouble for both our people. If it were just between you and me, it would be done the right way. But knowing that it won't be only us trying to make this work out, we both have doubts about it being done correctly."

Lily started to say that she felt that Mike would be one who could truly help direct his people to do what was right for both sides. But as she started to explain her reason for this, something happened. There was a lot of loud yelling outside the tent that meant that there was a problem occurring. So they all stood up and went outside to see some fighting going on. Mike and Fox started telling their people to stop the fighting now. Some of them did stop, but others continued. Mike and Fox pulled them apart from each other and yelled at them to quit the fighting.

When they finally stopped, Mike asked, "What started this fighting? And who was involved in the beginning of it?"

A native woman with her son came forward. The boy had a cut on his forehead and his face was badly bruised.

Fox and Lily went over to the woman and asked the boy what had happened, and he said, "I was just walking around when I saw a horse. He was wandering about, with no one with him, so I went over to the horse. As I was talking to him and petting his head, I was grabbed from behind, and thrown aside. I fell to the ground and hit my head on a rock. When I stood back up onto my feet a soldier asked me why I stole the horse. When I told him that I did not take him, he started to hit me hard on my face. The soldier started yelling at me, calling me a liar, and a thief. He was about to hit me again, but Raven stopped him. That's when the fighting started."

Mike then asked, "Who was the soldier that hit you?"

When the boy pointed his finger at him, Fox recognized him. The soldier walked forward toward them. He was the same soldier that Fox already had two conflicts with.

Fox asked, "Did you see this boy take the horse or did someone else?"

"We don't need to see a thief when you're surrounded by them."

Mike told the soldier that he did not answer Fox's question. Mike then asked him, "Who was standing guard over our horses?"

Another soldier stepped forward and said he was and that he didn't realize one was missing until now.

Mike asked, "Did you witness any horses acting afraid or different while you were guarding them?"

"No. I did not. But when the fighting started they became excited and hard to keep calm."

Mike then went over to the boy, looked straight into his eyes and said, "Young one, you do not have to be afraid of me. I will not hurt you no matter what the truth is. But I do need to know for sure that what you have said is the truth."

"You can ask Raven, because he was near me when I saw the horse, and I went to him." Raven was on the ground and not moving, so Lily went over to him. She tried to move him with her hand under his back, but when she felt something wet. She removed her hand from under him. She stared at her hand because it was covered with blood. She felt his chest and rolled him over and saw a knife wound in his back, and Raven was dead because of it.

Mike looked at the soldier and asked him if he killed that warrior. The soldier's reply was no he didn't. But Mike knew that he was lying, so he ordered his men to place him under arrest and to take away all his weapons. "You are going back to the fort to stand trial for murder."

"You can't do that to me, because you do not have any proof that I killed that savage." Mike then told his men to place him in restraints, and to go to camp and tell the others to get ready to leave. He turned to Lily and Fox and told them that he would make sure that justice was done for what had happened here.

Mike then went over to the boy and touched his shoulder and said, "Son you did the right thing by trying to help the horse, and I thank you. I know this soldier was wrong with his words and also his actions. But please don't judge all soldiers as bad people because of what has happened here. A warrior of yours, that I met a while ago, has opened my eyes to many things. He told me that I would face an evil happening at another time in my life. And that I must follow my true inner self in order to make it to be right, and not wrong this time. He was a man like no one else I have ever known or ever will. In the short period of time I spent with him, my life has been given a whole new meaning and I have a new outlook on things. He told me that my purpose was to help life, to remain strong with goodness, when facing things that were wrong. Please, son. Do the same; do not let what's happened here today turn you bad, by wanting revenge."

As Mike started to walk away, Lily thanked him for his kindness of heart, and said, "The warrior that you spoke of is an individual that we know too. Do you know what his name is, Mike?"

"Yes, Lily. He has a name that represents exactly who he truly is; the Warrior of Truth."

"Mike, we do know him, and I am very happy to see that

your soul has been touched like Fox's and mine by him. He may not be here in person, but once your spirit, and his, have connected, you will always be together. I hope the next time we meet, it will be a much better time. Be careful and continue to follow your new life because it is a good one."

Morning Mist and I were walking the mountain. I was going to take her to my place of birth; the oak tree cave. When we went inside and sat down, I started telling her about White Cloud. We were talking about my mother when all of a sudden the cave walls began to glow brightly. I could tell that Morning Mist was a little frightened because she wasn't sure what was happening.

I reached out and held her hands and said, "My love, I understand that this experience is something that you have not learned about fully yet. There is nothing to be afraid of. The spirit that is coming to us will be my mother and she is coming here to help us both. She is going to speak to you about me, and she may say some things that might hurt you. I will be here at your side, to help you to understand what she is saying. I have been telling you and explaining to you already about what she will be speaking about. Her main reason for doing this is to bring you more strength and understanding about what is to be when the time is right. She is also doing it to show you that she will always be there for you, just as Red Feather and Running Deer are. When you are in need, just ask, and you will receive them and their help. There are also others who will, but the ones who are your family, will be the closest and easiest to contact. So remain strong and open yourself up to the light that brings truth, goodness, and righteousness. Your destiny is what it is and it can be difficult at times to understand why it has to be that way. But always remember no matter what it is, that love is the correct answer to it all. Love will give you the strength to continue in the correct direction, in your life."

My mother, White cloud, came into full view. She was beautiful, standing in the center of the bright light.

"Mother, thank you for coming to us. It is wonderful to see you again."

"I have come to you because Morning Mist needs to be reassured that she can do what will need to be done, when the time is right. First I would like to say that I can't wait to see the birth of my granddaughter. We are all excited for the two of you. Running Deer, Red Feather, Peace, and I know that this child will have true love forever.

"Morning Mist, I do know that there will be times in your life that you will have hard thoughts about certain things, which will be happening. But always know that we all will be at your side, to help guide you, and protect you, through this period of time. When you become confused and unsure of the correct answer to your questions, take a look into your inner soul and you will have the right answer. My son will also be at your side and his daughter will be to, forever."

"White Cloud, why are you telling me that something in the future is going to be hard to accept? Because I get the same feeling from Warrior of Truth but he won't tell me what it is. Will you please tell me, so that I can be prepared for it?" asked Morning Mist.

"Morning Mist, there will be a time when you will be asked to do some thing that will be a very painful and difficult thing to do. My son and I are preparing you for this, by explaining to you how important it is for you to do it, because it will need to be done. You will know when that time has come, but for now, you need to take each step with strength, courage, and love. The one thing that I want you to always remember is this; my son's love for his people and all life here on Mother Earth is very special and strong. But his love for you and his daughter, is even stronger then any other love."

"Mother, I know that you know this, but I also love all of you as well, and I thank you all for everything given to me," said the Warrior of Truth.


Fox and Lily new that they had to go to Buffalo Tear to tell him all about what had happened. Fox told Lily to remain at the village while he went to see Buffalo Tear. When he arrived at Buffalo Tear's village, Fox explained to Buffalo Tear about the incidences. Buffalo Tear asked Fox to stay and wait for him to return, because he was going to gather some other villagers and bring them back so that they could also hear the story about what had happened.

He first went searching for John. When he found him, he asked him to go to his hut and wait with Fox. Buffalo Tear then crossed the mountain stream and opened his inner self up, so that he could locate Morning Mist and me. When he came to us he stood there quietly waiting because he didn't want to interrupt us. I knew he was there waiting and so did my mother because she looked at him, and waved to him as she left. Morning Mist and I stood up and walked over to Buffalo Tear.

"We will go with you, Buffalo Tear, to your hut, because

together we will help John to understand what his task is going to be."

As we were walking down the mountain, Morning Mist asked many questions about how Buffalo Tear and I were able to know things before others.

Buffalo Tear answered her by saying, "Because a gift from the Creator has been given to us to help life here on Mother Earth. There are also others out there that have this gift, and they to have it to help things to be right. There are some who have it, but they are frightened by it because it can be difficult to understand at times. When one learns that they do have a purpose here, and that there is a reason for all the things that do happen. The Warrior of Truth, me, along with some others, walk Mother Earth to keep life safe. We also try to help life to see its true meaning. There are many different emotions that can be felt. The emotions that are wrong can be overpowering to the emotions that are good.

"When that does happen, there will be destruction, pain, and incorrect change done. As long as people walk Mother Earth there will always be wrong, and it will have to be confronted. The ones who allow bad and wrong emotions to take control over them, is the reason for me, your loving man, and some others, to be on Mother Earth at the present time, for life's protection. If there is a time when bad and wrong is all that is left on Mother Earth, life here will end because our Creator of life will not allow evil to be a part of him."

When we reached the stream we held each other's hands as we walked across it to the other side. We went straight to Buffalo Tear's hut. When we entered it, John and Fox were both talking to each other. We all sat down next to them and Fox told us all about what had happened at his village. John was very upset about the fact that Mike had said that his officials were going to try and make agreements about land and trading material items. John felt that this meant that his people figured that the land that the natives lived on belonged to them, and not the natives.

John said, "My people are going to try and use material things to convince you and your people to move to an area of less importance to them. I have a feeling that this new area will be a place that is worthless. You may have very little water, animal life, and fertile soil."

We all talked about the fact, if our people would resist the agreements that they offered, we would be considered enemies to them and war would begin between us.

John's heart was filled with sadness as he spoke, "I have to go to Mike and find out who these higher up people are and try to talk to them. I wish I could say that they will do what I ask them to do. But I can't say for sure if they will even allow me to meet with them." I then said to John, "I understand what you are saying so I want you to know this. Do not ever give up on anything that you know and feel is the right thing to do. You have become one of us and you know what must be done and the reason for it. I am honored that you are going to speak to your people on our behalf. When you get the chance to speak, some of your people will listen to you and they will see it as you do. But there will be others who will not and they will try to make you look like a fool. You remain strong and continue to follow your true inner self because this is the reason you have come to us. I know that you will give all of yourself to your people, to help them to see what should be done right. Thank you for all that you are about to do for us, my brother, and always know that you are apart of us too."

Buffalo Tear handed John a medicine pouch and told him
to carry it with him always, for protection and strength.

We all hugged him and I said this to him, "You will be
known to our people as the White Warrior from this day forward." Morning Mist thanked him for his love, Fox said he
was honored to have met him, Buffalo Tear said he too was
honored.

And I said, "White Warrior, you will not go alone when
you have your meeting with those leaders. Mike will be with
you because he to wants to help make things to be right." We
all walked together to the two horses that were waiting for Fox
and John.

They rode together back to Fox and Lilly's village talking
about different ideas to solve some of the problems coming.
When they arrived Fox asked two of his warriors to escort
John back to the fort, to make sure that he returned there
safely.

Morning Mist and I went back to our mountain home and
talked for a long time. We were both very happy about our
child, but she was worried about her. She was afraid that the
world she was being born into would be one of great unrest.
I helped her to understand that she needed to be our child's
strength and insight to love. With tears in her eyes she then
asked me a question that I knew she had wanted to ask me
before. And I knew that I had to answer it as truthful as I
could.

She said, "During some of our conversations at times, the
words that you had said to me made me think that you may
not be around to help me raise our child."

"Morning Mist, I talked to you like that because of all the problems that our people are going to have to face. I do know what my purpose and destiny is on Mother Earth. I can not tell you exactly when my physical body will no longer walk Mother Earth because I don't want you to feel that pain now. There is a time when all physical life forms do leave. I have explained to you that our people will soon be facing some serious challenges. "When this does happen I cannot bring you, Morning Mist, and our daughter with me. Because of the danger that I will need to face, I want you to know and accept this fact. If you ever lose my physical body, please know that I will always be with you and our daughter spirituality, watching over you both, protecting, and giving you both strength with my love."

Morning Mist and I held each other tightly together in our arms. I could feel her love and also her fear of losing me. While I held her close to me, I asked our guardians to please help keep her strong when my time does come. And to always protect her, and my daughter, and guide them through the difficult times that were coming.

John and the two warriors were only two days out of our village when they came across an area where a fight had taken place. It was a small Indian village that had been attacked. There were no human bodies found, but there was a lot of blood on the ground which showed them that death did occur.

There were a few dead horses, some were native horses and others were white men's because they had saddles on them. John and the two warriors knew they needed to remain alert, that there could be danger waiting for them. They continued to travel toward the fort and after a few more days, it came into view. John thanked the warriors and hoped they would have a safe trip back to their village. The warriors wished him good luck and headed back toward their village.

When John entered the fort he asked the soldiers at the gate if he could see Colonel Luken. As they were bringing him to the Colonel, John saw Mike walking. When John yelled hello to him, Mike came running over to John. They shook hands and began to talk about the incident at Fox's village. Mike then told John about the soldier he had returned with to be put on trial.

Mike said, "When the trial was over the soldier was found not guilty and released back on duty. And during the trial they made me look like the one responsible for what had happened because I took the side of the Indians. Colonel Luken transferred the soldier to another fort because he was disappointed with the procedure and the verdict. Now because of his actions the high up officials are trying to remove the Colonel Luken from here."

John then told Mike the reason why he had returned to the fort. That he was going to go to the capital city to speak with the main officials in charge because he felt that what they were doing to the native people was not correct.

Mike then said, "Let's go to Colonel Luken now because I think maybe he can help you."

They both went to the colonel's office and spoke to him about what John was going to try to do. Colonel Luken was glad to see John. He was excited to hear that he wanted to talk to the officials who were causing the big problems. Colonel Luken said that he would like to go with John, but that he couldn't because he was needed on the front line. He felt that if he left his position that worse things could and also would happen to both sides.

Colonel Luken asked Mike if he would like to join John in his mission of peace. Mike was grateful that the colonel had asked him go with John. The colonial told them both to please stay in contact with him so that he could maybe help them out there. Colonel Luken gave John and Mike the names of some of the officials he knew. He told them that they would listen to them and that they may also help support their ideas. The three of them spent the next couple of days together preparing themselves for the difficult quest at hand.

# CHAPTER EIGHT

Morning Mist and I spent our time together on the mountain. She was much stronger now because I showed her how to know her soul and protect it from things that were bad. Our child inside her was also the reason for her becoming stronger with strength. We both knew that at her birth, the two of us would have such a special gift of love, to always protect. It was a wonderful experience to feel her movements and to see her growth inside Morning Mist. Every part of Morning Mist would be that of our child's as well. Our child's true soul would also be connected to others who walked Mother Earth, before her time.

All of life is connected and it has been since the very beginning and it will be to the very end. She will be born into a time with a lot of conflict among the people on Mother Earth. But when she has learned to follow her true inner self, she to will become one also of goodness. All the wrong and bad that she faces will never have control over her and her life. Because her inner self will be the same as her mother's and mine. She will be true to all life. She will follow the path of goodness and righteousness because of who she is.

It was almost dawn when Morning Mist and I walked outside to watch the sun come up. The sky became active with falling stars. They all were bright white in color except one. As it went over us, the color was glowing bright red and Morning Mist felt our child was ready to be born. She lied down on to the sacred mountain. We both were very excited and happy to know that our child's time had come.

She was born as the sunlight started to brighten up the sky. I placed her in Morning Mist's arms and then held them both in mine. I thanked our Creator and our guardian angels for our baby's healthy birth.

Morning Mist and I had two names for our child and they both were good ones. One was Red Star, which honored her father, and the other was Morning Star, which I felt honored everything. Morning Mist and I talked about her name to be for a while. I told Morning Mist that I felt that Morning Star should be her name, because of its meaning: that Morning Star honored our sun, moon, stars, sky, Mother Earth, and all life. The red falling star was the beginning of her birth, and the morning sun was her new life here on Mother Earth. Morning Mist agreed that Morning Star should be her name because of its true meaning. I picked them both up in my arms and carried them back inside our hut so they could rest.

Before sunset I carried Morning Star and her mother out to the ridge that over looked our village. I held Morning Star in my hands out in front of me to show our people our new baby girl. I then yelled out our daughter's name, "Morning Star," so that all our village people would know her name.

Buffalo Tear came running across the stream and up the

mountain so that he could hold our child in his arms. He was so full of joy when he held her next to his heart.

"Buffalo Tear, you now have a new young one to help watch over and guide. I know that you will always be there for both Morning's." Together we all laughed and held each other tight with love.


The next few years passed quickly and I loved every moment of them with Morning Mist and Morning Star. It was wonderful to hear her first words spoken and to see her first steps taken on Mother Earth. Morning Star's words someday will have great meaning to all life and she will walk Mother Earth with great strength. Knowing this made me very happy inside because she too was going to be a protector of all goodness in life.

The conflicts between the whites and us were becoming much worse. The time had come and we were now at war with them. And this meant that our ways of life would soon be totally different for us. Many of our villages and people had been destroyed. The ones who survived were placed on reservations and controlled by the white people's ways. The freedom we once had was no more, because the change was now happening. Many of the innocent white people were also killed because of the hatred and revenge from my people. I tried to make them see and understand that it was the wrong thing to do.

But then the time came; Fox and Lily with some of their people came to our village. They were recovering from an attack from white soldiers who were now coming to our village to do the same. Buffalo Tear wanted to go and meet them, but I told him that he couldn't. If he did go, I knew that he would be killed before he could even speak to them. So I asked him to please go to Morning Mist and Morning Star along with our people and continue to guide and protect their lives through this change. Buffalo Tear wanted me to go to the mountain because he knew what I knew and it was about to happen.

I wrapped my arms around him so he could see clearly that he needed to do what I said because our destiny is what it is. We both had to follow it now, no matter how painful it was going to be because it was the right thing for us to do. With tears in our eyes, but with strength in our souls, we separated and said, "Go with love to each other."

I turned to Fox and Lily and told them that I will go and try to stop this, but that I first needed to see Morning Mist and Morning Star. When I left, Fox told Lily that he was going to gather warriors and also try and stop the soldiers before they came to the village.

I went straight to Morning Mist and Morning Star and they were waiting for me. Morning Mist knew that something was happening because she saw Fox and Lily enter the village. I held Morning Star in my arms and I had a hard time letting go of her so that I could also hold her mother. I told her that I loved her and to always know that I will be there for her when she needed me. I then held Morning Mist in my arms and told her the same thing. She started crying very hard because she knew that the time had come that I had to do something important. I explained to her what had happened at Fox and Lily's village and that the soldiers were headed toward ours. That I now needed to leave and try to stop the soldiers before they did the same thing to our village, and our people.

"Buffalo Tear will soon be here to keep the two of you safe and protected. Remember that I will always be there with my love, to help and protect you both from evil, and its ways."

Morning Star came to us because she saw us both in tears. We held each other close for a long while before the feeling came to me that I had to go now because the soldiers were coming. The hardest thing in my whole life, on Mother Earth to do, was to release my loved ones from my arms. But I knew that I had to in order for me to save their lives, and also some others.

"I love you Morning Mist. I love you, my daughter. Carry my love with you forever." I turned and ran down the mountain, back to the village.

I stopped at the stream and waved to all my loved ones with my love so that they would know that my love for them was forever. I then ran to a horse and jumped onto his back with a heavy heart because of knowing what was to come.

Fox and a large amount of warriors were heading toward the soldiers. They all knew that they needed to stop the soldiers from reaching the village and the sacred mountain. My horse was running as fast as he could because he also knew that we had a mission to do.

When I came over a grassy knoll I could see the soldiers and also Fox and his warriors. They both were preparing to start fighting, but they noticed that I was coming. I thanked my horse for bringing me to them before the battle. As I continued to ride toward the soldiers, I knew my people were watching me, and that I needed to be stronger this time around than any of the others in the past.

Then there were many guns fired and my horse fell to the ground dead. I, too, had many bullet wounds in my body. But with inner strength I stood up on my feet and started walking toward the soldiers with only a quiver of arrows in my hands. They all fired their guns again and I fell to my knees when the bullets hit me. But again with strength from within me, I stood back up with my arrows in my hands above my head and yelled to them all.

"This is the wrong thing to do, stop this now and go home, all of you, so that no more innocent lives are lost." I broke the arrows in half and threw them at the soldiers. I dropped to my knees; my soul then left my body with a white wolf and white eagle at its side. When my people saw the white wolf and white eagle, with a streak of white light between them, they knew that I was no longer here on Mother Earth.

Fox and the warriors knew that the broken arrows meant that the battle was over and that they needed to return home like I said. So Fox and his warriors rode off toward the village. They all had tears in their eyes because of my death.

The soldiers were also stunned because they couldn't believe what they were witnessing and hearing. The white wolf, white eagle, and I, remained above my people as they rode away, to protect them. An officer came forward and said that they needed to go back to their fort to revise a new plan.

A soldier who was not an officer then said, "We need to attack them now because they're running away and we could get them all."

The officer asked, "Who gave the order to fire guns at the native who was alone and coming to us? Because I think he was going to try and negotiate with us."

The soldier then said that he did and then he started yelling loud and calling the officer a fool for not attacking those other Indians. The officer told the soldier that he shouldn't have given the order to open fire, that he was not the one in charge, that all he wanted to do was to kill the natives. And he knew this because he had read record reports about him and his past actions, which he had committed in other areas, and that was the reason way he had been transferred. The soldier became really mad. He was about to take another action against the officer, and the soldier grabbed his gun.

The soldier became so enraged with anger and hatred that he suddenly felt a sharp pain in his chest, the pain was so intense that it caused his heart to stop beating. He dropped dead to the ground with his gun in his hand. A wolf and eagle made a loud noise. The officer asked his men to remove the soldier's body.

Another soldier then came forward to the officer and said, "That man died the correct way because he was always doing bad things. He has killed a lot of Indians who were innocent, just like the last one here. But it looks like justice has finally caught up to him."

The sacred mountain animals all began to cry loudly. Buffalo Tear, Morning Mist, and Morning Star were together in the village when the mountain wildlife started crying. Together they all went over to the stream. The village people that were still there came running to the mountain stream too. They joined Buffalo Tear, Morning Mist, and Morning Star and together they all stood crying because they all knew that they had now lost the Warrior of Truth on Mother Earth.

I knew that I needed to do something, to help remove the pain and sorrow in their hearts. So I asked for some help from our Creator to give them peace. The sky color turned into the colors of a rainbow and created a circle around the whole mountain. Then three faces became visible to them all; mine, a wolf, and eagle. I wanted them all to feel and know that they needed to continue to follow the correct paths in their destinies. And that I would always be watching over them to help them during their journey on Mother Earth. This is the end of this story, but it is the beginning of a new one now.

**PART 2**

## WARRIOR OF TRUTH'S DAUGHTER, MORNING STAR, AND HIS SPIRIT FOLLOWER, "BUCK"

Morning Star was standing along side the stream at the base of the sacred mountain. It had been over twenty years since she had been able to return to her place of birth. Her hair was long, light brown in color, and braided on both sides of her face. She wore a beaded necklace that had three eagle feathers attached to it along with some small braided pieces of silver wolf hair. The necklace use to belong to her mother, Morning Mist, but now it was hers. She wore it always in honor of her mother and also her father.

There was no longer any sign that her people's village had once existed there. She wanted to come to her place of birth sooner, but she wasn't able to because of what was placed in her path of life to face. Her journey on Mother Earth so far had been one of many challenges.

Morning Star was drifting back in time in her mind to her childhood. It all began the day that Buffalo Tear, Morning Mist, Morning Star, and their village people were all standing at the same spot she was at. The sacred mountain was covered with white glowing clouds that turned into the colors of a rainbow. Three forms then took shape within the clouds; a wolf, an eagle, and her fathers, the Warrior of Truth. He spoke to them all in spirit form with words of strength, courage, and love in order for them all to continue their journey on Mother Earth without him in his physical body. He wanted them to see and know that he would always be there to help guide them, when they were in need of him, during their journey on Mother Earth.

She remembered her mother lifting her up into her arms, and seeing her mothers face, filled with tears. It caused Morning Star to feel pain in her heart because she had now lost both of her parents. She began to cry hard.

Suddenly a wolf began howling on the side of the mountain. She saw him standing on the mountain ridge where she had lived with her parents. There was also an eagle circling in the sky right above the wolf. She understood that it was a sign for her to go there, so she stepped into the stream to cross it. When the water touched her feet she remembered her mother and father beside her, holding her hands as they crossed the stream together. It brought tears to her eyes again because she missed them both being with her physically. But she knew that they were watching over her because at other times in her life, they had come to her spiritually, to help guide her. And she could feel them now holding her close to them in their arms, which gave her the strength to stop the sadness and crying.

She stopped walking and stood in the mountain stream because now in her mind she could see Buffalo Tear.

Buffalo Tear turned to speak to his village people when her

father and his totems vanished from sight. Buffalo Tear said that they were going to have to face many challenges of conforming to other ways of living in order for their survival to continue. He asked them to never forget their beliefs and ways of living because it was who they were at the present time. He said that he knew that some of them would forget and be totally different individuals, because of the changes coming, which could mean that their true inner selves could be lost forever in the time to come. He hoped that when a decision had to be made between right and wrong. That the choice made would only be the right one. Because when it is the wrong one, there will be pain and suffering felt for life.

Buffalo Tear told them that Warrior of Truth had fulfilled his purpose on Mother Earth by helping life to reopen their inner souls to the true meaning of life which is love, respect, goodness, and to follow your correct path with strength and courage. The Warrior of Truth would always try to help those in need of him, but in order to receive his help they would need to be open to him for his guidance. Buffalo Tear said that if you ask the Warriors of Truth for his assistance, whenever you are in doubt about a decision, he would help you make it to be the right one for you and also others. He said the Warrior of Truth would always be a part of everyone because they were also apart of his true soul, when he walked Mother Earth as well.

Buffalo Tear then said to please always remember to honor and respect the Warrior of Truth for returning to us the true meaning of life here on Mother Earth. And also for being here physically for us in our time of great need.

Lily and Fox walked over to Buffalo Tear and Fox asked him if he could tell their people about what had happened at the battleground to the Warrior of Truth. Buffalo Tear told him to please do so, because he wanted his people to always remember the strength and courage that is connected to doing what is right and good.

When Fox finished the story of what happened, Morning Mist and Morning Star held Buffalo Tear together in their arms. Lily and Fox went over to them and they also joined them with their hugs of love. Then the village people began to hug each other to show their respect, honor, and love, for the Warrior of Truth too because he had hugged them all with love, respect, and honor, many times before.

A few weeks had passed by at the village, then one day a soldier arrived there alone. He placed his guns on the ground and raised his arms straight up above his head and began to wave his hands. He did this to show the villagers that he came to them peacefully and that he would not harm anyone.

Fox and the other warriors recognized his actions because the Warrior of Truth had done the waving many times before so they allowed the soldier to enter the village. He asked to see Buffalo Tear because he had been sent there to them by a good friend. Fox escorted him to Buffalo Tear.

Morning Mist and Morning Star were sitting with Buffalo Tear talking about the future when Fox asked for permission to enter his hut.

With sadness in his voice and his head down the soldier spoke, "My name is Mike. I am sorry for your loss of a man of great value to us all. I knew him and I promise to always do and follow what he has shown and taught me. My best friend, who I consider a brother, also wants you to know that he will also do the same and he sends his regrets. John, who you have named the White Warrior, and I have been working with our government trying to get things done right for your people and ours. Some are following the correct path, but like the Warrior of Truth has told us, some will not. And they are the ones who seem to be influencing others to do things the wrong way, instead of the right way."

Buffalo Tear then said, "Mike, you and John are two individuals that the Warrior of Truth is proud of because the two of you are doing things the right way and you are trying to make others see and do what needs to be done correctly. Both of you are following your true inner souls and that is wonderful to see and feel. The two of you need to continue to be strong when faced up against those who do what is not right.

"I understand that it is difficult at times to accept things when you know that what is being done is wrong. But what is important is this; you must stay the path that is right and good. And don't be drawn to do something wrong because that means you have made what is wrong even stronger. I thank you, Mike, for everything that you and John have done to help us and also your people."

Mike stepped over closer to Buffalo Tear and lowered his voice and said, "There is something else that we need to talk about, Buffalo Tear. And I think that we should be alone because I know that your people will get upset if they hear what I need to tell you."

"Yes, Mike, we will talk, but I want Fox, Lily, Morning Mist, and her daughter Morning Star to be with us because they are an important factor in our future. It's coming soon."

Buffalo Tear already knew inside him what Mike was going to say to them. Because a while back, when he was at the sacred mountaintop with the Warrior of Truth, he had seen this happening then.

Buffalo Tear then felt the Warrior of Truth, speaking to him inside, just as he did back at that time too. He was telling him to follow his correct path and to remain strong because their people would need his strength and wisdom to be able to survive this outcome. Buffalo Tear asked Fox to find Lily and bring her back to them so that Mike could say what was needed to be said to them all.

Morning Star started to walk again in the water toward the mountain. She could see that something was moving in the tall grass by the stream bank. She knew that it was a wild animal of some kind, but she didn't feel afraid of it because she felt that it was another sign from her ancestors. This one was welcoming her to the mountain.

A mountain lion stepped out of the tall grass and walked out into the stream. He stopped and stared at Morning Star. She took a few steps closer to him and stopped so that he could see and feel that she was no threat to him. The mountain lion responded to her reactions. He sat down in the water; this was showing Morning Star that he was not a threat either. Morning Star walked over to him slowly and held out her hand in front of his face. The mountain lion touched his nose on her hand and then lowered his head so that her hand now rested on the top of his forehead.

Morning Star began to pet the top of his head, which made him start purring with joy. They both were excited and happy to be with each other. Morning Star felt the same joy when she first saw him exit the tall grass because she remembered that Buffalo Tear once told her that one of her totems was a mountain lion.

He had explained to her what the meaning of the mountain lion totem was. It is the power of protection and teaches you to take charge of your life in order for you to make the right decisions when they are needed to be made. The mountain lion totem would also give you the strength and courage to face any kind of struggling events that could cause pain and suffering in your life.

Morning Star had seen other mountain lions before, but today was the first time she was ever able to touch one physically.

The mountain lion stood up in the water. Together they walked across the stream toward the mountain. When they stepped out of the mountain stream, Morning Star went to her knees to thank her ancestors and guardian spirits for allowing her to return to her place of birth and home. The mountain lion came over to her side and sat down next to her. She reached out and wrapped her arms around his upper body and held him close to her. Together they were showing each other the love, respect, and honor that they felt for each other.

They then heard the sound of many guns being fired in the distance. They both stood up and ran into the mountain forest to hide from who ever was doing the shooting. When she felt that they were safe, she stopped running and walked over to a small ridge on the mountainside to see if she could see what was happening.

There was a group of soldiers on horses chasing some of her people, and they were heading toward the mountain. When her people reached the mountain stream they crossed it and rode their horses down stream away from her. But then she saw a few of her people head into the forest at the base of the mountain while the others continued to go along the mountain stream.

When the soldiers reached the mountain stream a few of them crossed the stream and continued to chase the Indians. The other group of soldiers, on the other side of the mountain stream, also headed down stream away from her. She knew that the ones on the far side were going to try to circle around and try to get in front of her people. As the soldiers on her side of the stream rode by the area were she had seen some of her people go into the forest.

Morning Star saw the soldiers at the back of the group start falling off their horses. There were arrows in their bodies. She saw her people come out of the forest and chase down the remaining soldiers. The soldiers didn't even realize yet that they were being killed off by Indians behind them.

Soon she could no longer see the fighting because they had ridden out of sight but she did hear guns being fired again. The mountain lion began to move around, but then he stopped and looked at Morning Star. When he saw that she was looking at him he began to move again. Morning Star knew that the mountain lion was trying to get her to follow him, so she did. Together they made their way up the mountain and after a short ways she realized where they were headed. It was the place on the mountain where she had lived with her parents. The hut that her village people had built was gone and the area had changed its appearance a lot. On the ridge that had overlooked her village, there were now small trees growing, along with some thick brush. But there were still some spots where her mother's wild flowers were growing. Morning Star made her way over to the edge of the ridge and looked out over to where her village use to be. There was no longer any sign that her people had once lived there. The mountain lion came over to her side, together they sat down, and she closed her eyes to rest because she was tired. They were natives of her race.

When the soldiers on the other side of the stream heard the sound of guns being fired, they crossed the stream and headed toward the shooting. The Indians were killing most of the soldiers because they had ambushed them. But when the other group of soldiers arrived the fighting became more intense and the Indians were now losing the battle. Two warriors were able to escape during the fighting and the soldiers had seen them get away. But they couldn't go after the two warriors because of their wounded soldiers and the fighting still happening.

When the fighting was over, the officer in charge had his men help the wounded soldiers to their horses. He knew that they needed medical attention soon, so they left the area.

After a couple of days of traveling they came to a town and asked for their help. The doctor there was able to save some of them, but there were some soldiers too far gone and he could not save their lives. The officer in charge asked the town's sheriff if he knew of anyone who could help them to track down two natives which had escaped the battle. The officer wanted to capture the two natives because of all the death that they had caused. He told the sheriff that they had been after this group of Indians because they had killed the supervisor and some others at a place called the Berry Reservation.

The sheriff told the officer that he knew of a man who might help them. That he worked for a local farmer and that he had helped guide wagon trains and other individuals to locate the areas they were traveling too.

The sheriff said, "His name was Bert, and when he was a

child his family was killed by an Indian raid at their home. He was captured and taken back to an Indian village, where he grew up, so he knows all about them, and their ways. Bert is also very knowledgeable about the land and he has done a lot of good things for people here. If you show him respect and honesty, Bert will do the same too you."

The sheriff told the officer to go north and that they would find the farmers land only after a short ways out of town. Because of the farmland being such a very large area, they would see a lot of wagon trails, fences, livestock, and employees working. And that the owner of the large farm was also the founder and owner of most of the town.

When Morning Star closed her eyes she returned in her mind to the past. Mike was talking to Buffalo Tear, Fox, Lily, Morning Mist, and her. Mike explained to them that his government officials were going to take their land from them. That they were going to send a company of soldiers, with a negotiator, to try to get their land from them with out any battles taking place. Mike also told them that he and the White Warrior had tried to make his government, not do this because of the sacred mountain and its special meaning to the natives living their life's here.

Mike said, "Some of our people understood and accepted what we had told them about this area and its people. But some of our government officials now want your land even more. They feel that they have no control over you and your people, or me and John now. So they began to do and say things to make John and me look like fools and liars. Eventuality they did convince some others to follow their ideas of what they wanted; your land and control. And that is why I am here now to inform you because they will be coming here soon for you and your land. They will want to take you and your people to a new area to live. It will be a reservation and there you will have many limitations and new rules to follow. I am sorry for this having to happen. John and I only hope that you and your people remain safe from any harm. If you allow me to stay with you, I will help you during the negotiations."

Buffalo Tear, Fox, and Lily knew that they needed to tell their village people that the soldiers were coming so that they wouldn't start a battle. So they gathered everyone in the village and held a meeting. The three of them tried to make the villagers accept and understand, what they were about to face. After they finished explaining what Mike had said, some of the villagers gathered their family and left the village. They did not want to go to a reservation and live the rest of their life there. They wanted to remain free as they always had been since their birth on Mother Earth.

After a few days, the soldiers did arrive at the village. Mike and Buffalo Tear went to them to talk. While they were speaking to each other the soldiers completely surrounded the village. They were acting like they were going to attack it.

Fox and Lily looked up at the mountain where Morning Mist and her daughter lived. They could see them standing on the ridge watching what was happening to their village.

Mike, Buffalo Tear, and an officer were walking over to Fox and Lily, when all of a sudden a gun was fired. Mike was hit with a bullet in his left arm. Now because of the gun being fired the village people were preparing to defend themselves. The officer who was with Buffalo Tear and Mike was the commanding officer of the soldiers. He started to yell at his soldiers not to shoot any more guns. But then the officer, who was known as Colonel Luken, fell to the ground with an arrow in his chest.

Buffalo Tear knew that his people did not shoot that arrow. Now Buffalo Tear and Mike realized that this action was one that someone else had planned to happen.

The soldiers all began shooting their guns at the village people. Fox and Lily were able to get to Mike and Buffalo Tear. The four of them were yelling to everyone to stop the fighting, but the soldiers would not stop because most of them thought that the natives had killed their colonel. This would mean that the fighting would continue and that the ones who had planned this to happen might win. Buffalo Tear, Mike, Lily, and Fox, made there way back to Buffalo Tear's hut, and they went inside.

Morning Star and her mother had witnessed everything that had happened. They saw the soldiers surround the village, and a group of others working there way into the village. When Buffalo Tear, Mike, and a soldier were walking, she saw one of the soldiers in her village shoot at them. They then saw another soldier shoot an arrow into the soldier's chest who was yelling for them to stop fighting. Morning Mist held Morning Star in her arms and began crying because of seeing her people, women and children, killed. She started asking for help from her ancestors and guardians to stop this terrible action.

After a few moments the sacred mountain began to tremble and the sky overhead turned dark in color. Then lightning came flashing down from the heavens and began striking the battleground. Some of the ones fighting were hit by the lightning. The soldiers that were mounted on horses lost control of their horses. Some of the soldiers were thrown to the ground. The soldiers that remained on their horses had to hold on tight with both hands, which meant that they couldn't do any fighting. With the earth trembling and the lightning striking the ground, the fighting was stopping. Everyone knew that they needed to find a safer place to be at. All the soldiers began retreating away from the village and the Indian survivors were moving to the mountain stream.

Buffalo Tear, Mike, Fox, and Lily left the hut and joined their survivors at the mountain stream. Morning Mist and Morning Star came down off the mountain to also join their people.

Buffalo Tear began to speak, "What has just happened here was a gift of protection to us from our ancestors. What we need to do now is this…"

He looked at Mike and said, "This man will take us to a place that he knows of which will keep us safe. If we were to stay here or try to go somewhere else, instead of with Mike, these soldiers along with some others will track us down and destroy us all. Our ways of life and living it are now going to have to change in order for us to remain on Mother Earth.

"Those of you who wish not to go with us may leave. I only hope that you do not have to suffer any more pain. I wish you well during the rest of your journey on Mother Earth. Please always remember our beliefs and our ways of life and teach your new born and young ones it so that we are not totally lost in time, because of the changes that are to come to us now."

Only a couple of villagers did leave, but most of them stayed with Buffalo Tear. He was sad to see his people leave his side because he would not be with them when they needed him to help guide them.

Mike then spoke, "We are going to have to travel a long ways away from here to another fort that I know of. I honestly think this whole action here was a setup to eliminate Colonel Luken and also Buffalo Tear. Morning Mist has told me what she saw and I am glad that the bullet hit me and not Buffalo Tear. I understand way you want me to do this for you and your people, Buffalo Tear. I promise to do everything that I can to keep your people safe with my people. But I do wish that you could remain here because I now know that this place is your home and that it is of great meaning and importance to you."

Buffalo Tear touched Mike's shoulder and said to him, "A while back in time, the Warrior of Truth and I were shown this day. And it was very difficult for me to accept it then, but it is what it is. So we will go with you to our new home, Mike. Thank you for your respect and being a man who is following the right path in life."

"I know, Buffalo Tear, that my life has a purpose here on Mother Earth and the man that taught me that is still at my side. I only wish that I could physically see and touch him because he opened my true soul up to me when I was blind of it."

After a few weeks of traveling Mike and Buffalo Tear located a place that they felt could be a safe area for everyone for a while. Mike asked them to stay there and wait for him to return. He was going to continue on toward the fort and make contact with them there, to make sure that it was safe and also the correct place to be at.

When Mike arrived at the fort he went straight to the commander in charge to talk to him. Mike wanted to make sure that he would be a person who would be honest and do things correctly. They talked together about all that had happened at Buffalo Tear's village.

Colonel Berry, the commander, told Mike that he agreed that what had happened at Buffalo Tear's village was not right. And that it would be difficult to prove who the ones responsible for it were. Mike told the colonel that he had a witness who actually saw the soldiers start the fighting by shooting a gun and bow. But they both figured that no one would believe the truth because the witness was a native. The colonel said that he would write up a report and send a copy of it to his higher-ranking officials. So that the ones who were responsible for what had happened at Buffalo Tear's village would now know that what they had planned was not a secret any longer.

Mike was glad to see that the colonel was a good man and that he was going to help Buffalo Tear and his people. Mike sent John a copy of the colonel's report; he also sent him his complete story of what had happened during his time with Buffalo Tear and also Colonel Berry.

When John received the information he went to other government officials and explained to them what had happened at Buffalo Tear's village. John asked them for permission to set up a reservation for Buffalo Tear and his survivors. He also recommended Mike to be the individual in charge of the reservation, because he knew that Mike would be a good person to keep both races at peace, by doing things right.

The government officials agreed to his requests for the reservation and Mike, but they also wanted John to go there to help set it up properly. They told John that when the project was completed he was to return back to his office because they were planning on setting up a new position. And that he would be the one elected to be in charge of it because he was a man doing good things, and right things, for people.

John sent a message to the fort for Mike. Mike was very happy to hear that John was on his way there to them and that Buffalo Tear and his people would be taken care of. Mike told Colonel Berry that John was on his way to help setup an Indian reservation. The colonel said that he would also help them to do whatever they needed done, so that everything would be done in a peaceful way.

When John arrived at the fort, Mike and John held a meeting with Colonel Berry and some of his officers. They talked about Buffalo Tear's people and how good they were and where they were staying at now. They discussed the location as being a good place to set up the reservation because it was a secluded and safe area for them and also the white people. Everything seemed to be working out in a good way at the meeting for Buffalo Tear's people.

The colonel said that his fort would provide the reservation with food, clothing, and protection from any intruders. He also said that he looked forward to meeting Buffalo Tear and his people, but that he would wait until they were settled down at the reservation before coming out to see them.

Mike and John thanked Colonel Berry and his officers for doing what needed to be done correctly for Buffalo Tear and his people. John also told them that now that they have shown their respect, they will also see it in return from Buffalo Tear and his people. Mike and John left the fort in the morning to return to Buffalo Tear and his people's new home. After a few hours of travel they arrived there. Buffalo Tear, Morning Mist, Morning Star, Fox, and Lily, along with the rest of Buffalo Tears people were glad to see the White Warrior and Mike return. Mike and John explained to them that this location was going to be their new home. They were all happy, but they all knew that the time had come to them for a different way of living.

## CHAPTER TWO

Morning Star opened her eyes because she heard an eagle calling out; he was circling above her in the blue sky. She then heard a wolf howling on the top part of the mountain too. So she and the mountain lion stood up and started to walk toward the direction of the howling wolf. Morning Star knew that the wolf and eagle were signs from her guardians to continue moving to the mountaintop. As she was walking through the forest the feeling of strength, happiness, and joy came to her heart and soul. It was a wonderful feeling for her to be back to her true home after all these years of being away from it.

When she reached the top of the mountain she went straight over to the rock ledge that she had stood on before. The view from the mountaintop was beautiful, just like it was when she was only a child. She could see for many miles in all directions, completely around the entire mountain. She remembered coming to this place on the mountain with her mother and father. The love she was feeling from them now was as strong as it was back then. She could feel their presents, but they were not visible to her. Tears began to form in her eyes because she wanted to not only see them, but she wanted to hold them both close to her.

The eagle flew down from the sky and landed on the ground. The wolf came over and laid down on the ground by the eagle. Then the mountain lion walked over to the two of them and he sat down next to them. Morning Star turned and looked at the three of them next to each other. She felt and also knew that this was another sign given to her, so she sat down and waited to see what was going to happen next.

A white cloud was coming down from the sky and began settling down on the ground between her and her animal guardians. After a short time, there was a form of a woman beginning to take shape inside the cloud.

The woman stood looking directly at Morning Star and she spoke, "It is wonderful to see you, my granddaughter. I know it is the first time you have ever seen me, but I have always been at your side, my dear, along with your other guardians and loved ones. Your mother and father have asked me to come to you, because my life on Mother Earth was a lot like yours has been so far.

"We both have had to conform to others, their customs, and ways, but that does not mean that you have to give up your true inner soul. Who you truly are inside should never be lost or given up no matter how much change one has to face or accept in order to survive here on Mother Earth. We both know the misery and pain that are felt from things that are wrong and evil. But when you go to your true soul you can always rise above it and defeat it from affecting you. If you don't defeat it and brush it away from you, it will only make you weaker and more susceptible to it. And that will only bring you down even more. You have learned what is needed for our people to do in order for them to continue believing in our ways and living along side the white people."

Then Morning Star spoke to her grandmother, "White Cloud, my father told me all about you and how wonderful you were in life on Mother Earth. I am honored to have you being a part of my true soul and me. Thank you for protecting me and watching over me. My father and Buffalo Tear have also explained to me what you have just said to me about my true soul. I understand that the strength is within me; it's just sometimes very hard to bring it out quickly enough to face the wrong things that are done. I have lost my father, my mother, and Buffalo Tear, along with some others that were very special people to me here on Mother Earth. I do understand that when it is our time to leave here, there is nothing that can be done to stop it from happening. But my question is, when evil and wrong is the reason for someone to leave, why is that allowed to happen?"

"Morning Star, you know the answer to that question because you are a part of it. And there are others who are also a part of that answer. Your heart, blood, and soul are all good and you are to continue doing what the others have left you with, within you. Your father, mother, Buffalo Tear, and the others that may have been taken from you and Mother Earth by wrong and evil. But their true souls were not, and their spirit will remain with those whom they have touched. This means that the strength of goodness and righteousness is still here on Mother Earth, and it will remain here as long as those with it continue to follow it.

"All things that happen on Mother Earth have a reason for it to be. When it is things that are bad and the reason for them is wrong, it needs to be corrected. It may take some time to correct it, because you may need to help others to see and understand the meaning of why it was a wrong doing. It will be a way to stop the wrong from over powering what is suppose to be right. What is right, and what is good has to eventually defeat that which is not or all life here on Mother Earth will lose."

"So you're telling me, White Cloud, and some others, that our purpose is to continue doing what our loved ones did to battle all that is wrong. I will and I feel that there are others that will as well. But I am sure that we are not as strong as the ones who have been taken from us. My Father and Buffalo Tear were two individuals with strength like no one else. So how can we defeat evil with out them?"

"The strength that they had has been passed on to you and also to the ones who believed in them. They no longer physically walk Mother Earth, but their spirits' strength does, and there will be others to come like them, to help keep the strength of evil down. They have shown you and taught you how to follow your true self, along with others, and that is where your strength is. Now you and the others must follow the correct path in your destiny, for it is your purpose and reason to be here on Mother Earth now."

Three more white clouds settled down next to White Cloud and then three more bodies began to take shape. The first one was Morning Mist, the next one was Buffalo Tear, and then there was a very bright white light circle, and her father, Warrior of Truth stepped forward to Morning Star, and he held her in his arms. "I love you, my daughter. And we are here for you because you and your life here on Mother Earth are in need. We know that you are having a hard time understanding and accepting the reason why things happen the way that they do. Love is the only feeling that you have that will give you the strength and courage to face all your challenges. We have come to you right now to add more love to yours, and this will help you to become stronger and more aware of the meaning of truth. You will be able to see and feel things much clearer now because of the new strength that our combined true love, will give to you."

Morning Mist, White Cloud, Buffalo Tear, and the Warrior of Truth formed a circle around Morning Star. They held each other's hands and tightened the circle so that they all were touching Morning Star. Morning Star could feel each one of them giving her their energy of love, along with their wisdom, courage, knowledge, and truth. She now felt that she had gained a much stronger spirit and soul from them.

"Thank you, my loved ones, for helping me. I feel so much better now. I now know and understand the reason why things are what they are and why they happen the way that they do. Living life without you all has been very difficult. I now know how to stay in contact with you, when I need to see and feel you, my loved ones.

"When I lost you, Mother, and Buffalo Tear at the reservation to that disease, I felt that I no longer wanted to be any part of those people there and their ways. But now I know that the people at the reservation were not the only ones responsible for the things that happened there. That there were other people above their authority controlling them, making them do things against us the way they wanted stuff done. Mike was a good man and he helped us a lot at the reservation. I was glad to see him and Lily join together as one. When he was promoted to a different job, and he and Lily left the reservation. It went down hill. We were no longer treated with any respect. Our food supply was terrible, and many different diseases caused a lot of sickness and deaths there. When the new supervisor in charge of the reservation was attacked and hurt by one of our kind, we all paid a price because of what happened. I wish that I had the strength, knowledge, and courage then to do something about correcting what was wrong."

"Morning Star, you do have the strength now and the truth. But back then you were not aware of it because it was being hidden from you and many others. The wrong and evil was strong, and it was controlling the feelings of most everyone involved in what was going on there. Your inner strength was weakened along with some others, because you allowed your physical emotions to take control over your true self. I am not saying that your physical emotions were wrong feelings, but I am saying that they were blind to meaning of the true truth of what needed to be right. You and the others needed to learn how to see wrong and evil when it is being deceptive. It is a dark energy source that is always present and you can see it only when you look at it from within your true inner soul with strength. Now you know how to, and you also know that it is time for you to do what it is needed to be done here on Mother Earth for life."

"Yes, father, I do. And I will teach others what you all have just given me because now I have the strength, courage, and knowledge. I promise you all that from this day forward I will do as you have done for all of life here on Mother Earth. And I know that you all will be there for me, to help guide me when I need your wisdom."

Morning Star hugged and kissed White Cloud, Buffalo Tear, and her mother and father. The wolf and eagle along with the other wild animals on the sacred mountain began calling out loud. The physical forms of Morning Star's loved ones were fading back to their spiritual forms. She raised her hands toward the heavens and thanked the Creator for sending her family to her. She said, "I love you all."

# CHAPTER THREE

Bert was repairing a wagon that had broken a rear wheel after it hit a hole in the ground. As he was working on it he saw some soldiers on horses approaching him from the distance. Bert was a tall, thin man with long black braided hair, that had a hawk feather placed in a braid. He was a white man, but he was raised in an Indian village. When he was only six years old, some renegade Indian warriors attacked his parent's farm. They killed his family, but they let him live so that they could use him as a slave at their village. As the warriors were returning to their village, another group of warriors confronted the renegades. The renegade warriors who killed his family were forced to give him to them, and he was lucky for that to happen, because theses warriors were from a village of good people.

Everyone at the village treated him with respect. He was treated as one of their own people because they felt that what had happened to his family was wrong. They helped him to grow up into adulthood correctly by teaching him, and also showing him, their love. Bert learned all about the native ways of living life, and their beliefs in it.

An old medicine man called Gray Owl took him under his wing; he helped Bert to become aware of his true self, and to follow the correct path in life. Gray Owl taught Bert that it was important for him to become a man who would do things right, when challenged by others that were doing them wrong. Bert learned from Gray Owl how to ask for help, and strength, from his spirit guardians when he needed it for guidance. Bert was at Gray Owl's side the day that he left Mother Earth. He told Bert that he would always be watching over him before he closed his eyes.

One day there was a village gathering and Bert was the reason for it. The villagers told him that they were all very proud of him for becoming a true and good man. They explained to him the reason why they were unable to return him to his white people when he was still only a child. It was because if they had done that then, they would have been the ones held responsible for his family's death, instead of the correct ones.

Bert was told that he was now a part of a new family and that he always would be even though his blood was white man's, not Indian. All the villagers accepted him and loved him for who he was and they all knew that he would always be a part of them too. They told him that he had grown up to be an individual that they trusted and respected. He had also shown them that he felt the same toward them. They said that they didn't want to lose him, but that now that he was an adult he would get the feeling of wanting to see, and also be with, his original people.

Bert was told that he was free to go to them whenever he needed to. But they asked him to please remain being the man that he was now, and not to change, because he was a person filled with goodness. His native family would remember him by his native name, Buck, because it was meaningful to him, Gray Owl named Bert, Buck, when he was a child.

Deer were animals that could adapt to the many changes in life. And that he was like them because he was able to adapt and accept the changes in his life, which also showed his strength and his ways of doing things right.

Three days after the village gathering, Buck was hunting food for his village people. As he was moving through a wooded area he heard the sound of something else moving around. It was making a lot of noise whenever it moved; it was stepping on twigs and other items that indicated to him that someone else was there. Buck stood still and waited for it to come into view. When he saw what it was he knew that he had to give himself to it, in order for it to survive. It was a white female child wondering around all alone in the wildness, which could be dangerous for her. So he took a step toward her, but when she saw him she became afraid and started to scream and run away from him. Buck realized that she was frightened of him because he looked like an Indian.

Buck started yelling to her and running after her, "Stop, little girl. I will not hurt you. I will help you to find your way back home to your family. I know that you are lost because you are way too young to be in these woods alone. Please listen to me and stop running because you could trip and fall and get hurt. I will stop running when you do, and stay away from you until you know that you can trust me. We will just talk and if you want me to help you to make things better for you, I will do that for you. My name is Bert and I promise to do whatever you ask of me to do."

She suddenly stopped running and turned to face him. Bert also stopped where he was to show her that he would do what he had said; he stood still waiting for her to speak to him.

"My name is Kathy, and I don't know where I am. And I am afraid of Indians. My mommy and daddy have told me to stay away from you because you kind of people are very dangerous."

"Kathy, please listen. Believe and trust me. I may look like I am an Indian but I am a white man. I have lived with them since I was your age. Some of them may be dangerous, just like some of our kind of people are as well. The Indian village that I grew up in is a place full of good and honest people. And they will always be a part of my heart because they have taught me to do things the right way. We have been brought together today for a reason. I will do everything that I can to get you back home to your family safely. You must know and feel that you need to be back home as well, so that you will make the right choices to get you there. I will be as happy as you, when I see you return to your family's arms again."

Bert heard the sound of a rattlesnakes tail shaking, and Kathy was about to scream and move.

"Kathy, do not move at all or scream because that snake will bite you. And if he does his venom could kill you or make you very sick. Be brave and remain quiet and still because he is near you. I will come to you and protect you from him."

Bert ran quickly over to her, the snake was near the back of her left leg ready to strike. So he stepped between her and the snake and the snake bit him instead of her. He grabbed the snake and smashed it against a tree, killing it. Bert then took the snake and rapped it tight around his leg, just above the bite. With his knife in hand, he began cutting deeply into the bite on his leg. Next he started squeezing the muscles around the bite to bleed out the snake's venom.

Kathy asked if she could do anything to help him because she could see that he was hurt.

"You can bring some small dry pieces of wood to me and I will start a fire. I will then singe this wound to purify and cleanse this snake bite." When he was finished with the procedure he was feeling exhausted because a small amount of the snake venom was still in his blood. Kathy started to ask him some questions.

"Do you think you are going to be alright? How long will it take to find my family and home?"

"I will be okay, but I need to rest and sleep for a while to regain my strength. Please stay here and don't wonder around. You get some rest too. When I wake up, we will start looking for your home. Can you tell me how you became lost, Kathy?"

"My grandfather wanted us to move west to his farmland. So my mom and dad found a group of others who were traveling together with wagons heading out west. They let us join them for most of the trip. But then one day we were told that we needed to go in a different direction than them. After a short ways we came to a river and as we were crossing it, the current caused our wagon to flip over into the water. And I haven't seen my mother and father since then."

Kathy started crying very hard and Bert could feel her sadness and pain. He had felt the same way when he lost his family to the renegade warriors.

"Kathy, we will go to your grandfather's place first. Because if your parents are still alive they will go to his place to get some help to find you. I'm sorry that this has happened to you and your parents. I want you to be strong and to think positive about what has happened. If you tell yourself that your parents are alive, safe, and not dead, you will be able to fulfill your needs to return to them. The love that you feel for them will give you the strength and courage to face any challenges on your way back to them. When you make the right choices you will go in the correct direction toward them. I have told you this already, but I am going to say it again. I promise to keep you safe and also to return you to your family. You can trust me, Kathy. I will do all that I can to make your life better for you."

As Bert closed his eyes to sleep, Kathy came over to his side and touched his hand and said thank you to him. While he was sleeping, Gray Owl appeared in his dream and began talking to him. He told Bert that he was proud to see him do things correctly for the lost child. And that another guardian spirit was also very proud of what he had done so far. Gray Owl had always talked about this warrior to Bert when he was young because he wanted Bert to become a good individual. Gray Owl touched Bert's shoulders with his hands and said, "Listen to him."

"I am the Warrior of Truth and I am very glad to see you following your true path on Mother Earth. You have done a wonderful and excellent procedure for this young one and I thank you for your honesty to her."

Bert had heard his voice before, but he had never seen the Warrior of Truth in any physical form. He had heard his voice many times when he was young and also as he became older. He wasn't sure who was making contact with him then, but now he does, and he felt honored to have been guided by the Warrior of Truth.

The sun was up high in the sky. Bert was still in a deep sleep when he suddenly felt the child touching his arm. When he opened his eyes Kathy was pointing her finger at something in the distance. Bert could see two men on horses with packhorses behind them. Both packhorses had many different animals hides piled onto their backs. He knew now that they were white men, called trappers. Back at his village he had seen many trappers like these two. They were white men from Spain, France, Britain, and other countries trying to trade things with the village people.

"Kathy, we have to be careful of them because they kill life for money and other items. I will try to speak with them to see if I can get any helpful information from them for you. What is your grandfather's name and do you know the name of the place where he lives?"

"William Thompson is my grandfather's name, and his farm is near a town called Sand Stone Creek."

Bert told Kathy to remain hidden, that he was going to go over to the trappers now and try to talk to them. His leg was still sore and stiff from the snakebite, but he started to run toward the two men. When the two trappers saw him running toward them, they drew their guns from their holsters and they were about to start shooting at him. They figured that he was an Indian and that he was after their animal hides.

Bert stopped running when he saw the two trappers draw their guns and point them at him because he knew that they were about to shoot at him.

He yelled to them, "I am a white man and I only need to ask you a couple of questions. I will stay right here so that you will know that I'm not after you or any of your stuff. Do you know of a place called Sand Stone Creek, or a man called William Thompson?"

The trappers kept their guns pointed at Bert, but they began talking to each other for a few moments. Then one of them said, "You speak English good and your skin does look like its white, but why do you look like a native? Is it because you live with them and you want us to answer your questions because you're up to something against us? If you take one more step toward us we will shoot your body full of bullets."

"I am helping someone who is lost in the wildness here, to return to their home safely. That is the only reason why I am standing here in front of you, asking you the location of Sand Stone Creek. Otherwise you would not even have seen me."

"Who is lost and how do we know that you're not just lying to us?"

Bert was about to answer him, but Kathy yelled at the two trappers instead.

"He is not lying to you. He is helping me so please tell him where Sand Stone Creek is so that I can go home."

Bert got the feeling that now that the two trappers knew there was a lost child. They would use her to receive more money. He knew that they were up to something because they were both talking to each other again, but they had their guns still pointed at him. So he turned around and started running back to Kathy. The two men began shooting their guns at him. He knew now that he was right about what he had felt about them, and what they would try to do.

Bert was moving around very quickly, and his running speed was so fast that none of their bullets hit him. When he reached Kathy's side he told her that they needed to get away from those two men because they were bad people. He looked back towards them to see what they were doing. One trapper was coming after them and the other one was no longer in sight. So Bert picked up Kathy into his arms and started running into a more dense part of the forest so that the one who was following them on a horse would have a difficult time riding after them.

After a short distance the forest became so thick with trees and brush that Bert had to slow down his running, and then he had to stop running. He showed Kathy a thick growing bush and told her to go and hide in it. He then climbed up into a tree near her and waited for the trapper to come riding by. The tree that he had climbed into was at a spot that the horse could only come through because of the density and height of the brush all around there. Bert could see the trapper on his horse riding slowly toward him. He grabbed a dead tree limb and broke it because he wanted the man to hear it break so that he would think that he was going in the right direction to catch up to them. The trapper did hear the limb break because he rode his horse right beneath the tree that Bert was in.

Bert jumped out of the tree onto the horses back behind the trapper. He held his knife near the trapper's neck and told him to drop the gun in his hand onto the ground.

When he did Bert got off the horse and put his knife back into its sheath and said to the man, "I could have taken your life because of what you have done so far, but I didn't. Does that tell you that all I wanted from the two of you was the answers to my questions? I did not want any of your material things, but you both were thinking that I did. Or did you think that if you killed me the two of you could return the child and collect a reward for her?"

Bert and the trapper now heard the sound of a gun being fired. Bert now had the feeling that the other trapper was in trouble. He asked Kathy to come over to him because he knew that there could be other problems to face. When Kathy came to him the trapper was staring at her because he didn't realize how young she was.

Then he said, "My friend was right. You did have others with you and you were after our hides and lives."

"No, I did not have others with me but you must have had others following or looking for you. And you were the ones who informed them of your location by shooting your guns at me. I know and understand that you would like to go to your friend and partner, but it is too late for that. You can go if you want to, but they will be waiting for you. I am sure that they know that there are two trappers and not just one. This means they could also still be looking to find you so you need to be cautious, and so do Kathy and I.

The trapper then said, "You are too young to be alone in this wildness, little girl. My friend and I didn't realize that you were only a child when we heard you speak. He figured that the two of you were after our stuff and also our lives so he wanted to kill you. I asked him to wait until we saw who the female's voice was, that we heard, but you turned away and started running. When he started to shoot at you, so did I, because now I believed that he was right about you. My friend took the packhorses and told me to follow you. Now that I see this child I know that we made a mistake by not answering your questions."

"Kathy and her family were traveling westward with a group of others by wagons. They were going to her grandfather's farm, but at some point they had to separate themselves from the others. Kathy's grandfather's farmland was located in a different direction of travel, then where the others were headed. They came to a river and while they were crossing it, the wagon overturned in the water. The fast current separated Kathy and her parents, and they haven't seen each other since. I am going to return her to her grandfather's. That is why I asked the two of you the location of Sand Stone Creek."

Now they heard the sound of not just one gun being fired, but many. Bert now had a feeling that the other trapper could be dead.

"Hearing that many guns shooting, tells me this, the ones responsible for your friend's death could be other whites or maybe natives."

The trapper then said, "My name is Dan, I am sorry that we made a mistake by shooting our guns at you. Now I realize that you were only trying to help this child. Do you think that we can go and see if my friend is still alive?"

"Dan, my name is Bert. We need to remain alert, and quiet here for a while, to keep Kathy safe. I think that the ones who attacked your friend are still out there searching for you. When the sun starts to go down we can make our way over to the area where we heard the gun fire."

Dan got down off his horse and stood still, because Bert reached down and picked up the gun on the ground. He then handed it back to Dan and told him to use it only to keep Kathy safe from any harm. Together they sat down with Kathy and rested. They waited for the sun to go down lower in the sky. While they waited, Bert explained to Dan how he was raised when he was a child, and that was why he looked like he did. When Bert felt that it was time for them to check out the area of the shooting, they made their way through the forest slowly and cautiously. As they came closer to the area, Bert told Kathy to remain there with the horse until they returned. He told her not to be afraid and to be patient and that he would be back soon.

The sun was down but the moon was up and it was a full moon, so there was plenty of light for Bert and Dan to see things clearly. The forest was opening up to a plains area. Bert could see a horse standing on the open plains in the distance by itself. He felt that the ones who were there before were now gone. He asked Dan to stay at the tree line while he went to see if he could get the horse. He knew that the horse could be helpful, traveling to Kathy's family. As he was walking out into the open plains he could see many horse tracks.

They were all running and he could tell that they were white men's horses because of the type of tracks. Native horses had no metal plates on their hoofs, but these did. And the horse that he was moving towards had a saddle on him, which also told him that it belonged to the whites.

Bert had a lot of experiences with horses and he understood their behavior. He knew that the horse was getting a little nervous by watching his reactions as he got closer to him. So he stopped walking and stood still so that he would calm down and not run away. After a short period of time he did calm down and he started to move toward Bert. Instead of running away from him because now he felt that he wasn't going to be hurt. When the horse stood in front of Bert, he began to pet his forehead and talked to him. Bert could see some blood on the horse, but it wasn't from any wounds he had. They were from his rider. Bert knew that the horse was acting afraid before because of what had happened to his rider, so he continued to pet and talk to him, to show him that he was safe.

After a while, he walked with the horse back to Dan. When Dan saw the horse up close he said that it wasn't his friend's horse because he was a different color and size. As they walked together back to Kathy, Bert told Dan that his friend was killed by other white men and not natives because of the things that he had seen. Kathy was glad to see Bert and Dan coming back to her. And she was also happy when Dan told her that he would help bring her to Sand Stone Creek in the morning.

Bert stayed awake while Dan and Kathy fall asleep because he wanted to watch over them and keep them safe. He looked up at the moon and stars in the night sky and said thank you to his guardians for helping him to keep Kathy safe from any harm during everything so far. He heard a voice speaking to him, within him. It was the one he had heard before, the Warrior of Truth.

"You have done everything correct and right so far. Your true soul is good and that strength will become stronger for you because you are following the right path in life on Mother Earth. Your guardians will always be there for you, to protect and help guide you. We all thank you for being your true self when things that are wrong challenge you."

Bert then saw three falling stars in the night sky. All three of them were going in the same direction. So he felt that it was a sign for him to go in that direction in the morning.

At sunrise Bert and Kathy rode together on one horse and Dan on his, in the direction of falling stars. After a short ways on the open plains they could see two bodies laying on the ground, so they went over to them. One was Dan's friend, and the other one was another white man. Dan got down off his horse and began to move some dirt with his hands to bury his friend's body. Bert got down off the horse and helped Dan cover the body. They were almost done, but Kathy told them that she could see some horses with riders coming toward them. Bert could tell that they were natives so he told Dan to stay with Kathy as he started running toward the Indians.

The group of Indians stopped and waited for him to reach them. When he made it to them he saw the pack horses that the trappers had, and also some wounded warriors, so he spoke to them.

"My native name is Buck. I want to speak to the warrior in charge here, please."

"He was killed by a group of white men, and he was my brother. I am Spotted Horse, you look native, but I can tell by your skin that you are not."

Spotted Horse jumped of his horse at Bert with his knife in hand. Bert moved away from him quickly and said to him, "I may not look like you because of my skin color, but I am like you. I was raised up from childhood, to adulthood, in a native village of good people. They are an important part of my life and they always will be. I know and believe in everything that they have taught me. I understand that because my skin is white you think that I am a threat to you, but I am not. If you want to fight me you can. I will only defend myself and that could mean that one of us could get hurt. You have lost your brother because of fighting and I am sorry that it happened. But I know and so do you that when fighting or battles occur pain is always felt."

"Buck, the words you have said to us are right. Who are the others behind you, waiting?"

"There is another white man and a young white girl who we are returning to her family. She was separated from her family because of an accident, and she has been wandering around in the wilderness alone. I feel that it is my responsibility to make sure she is reconnected with her family. Can you tell me why you attacked that group of white men? I hope that the animal skins weren't the reason."

"The animal skins were not the reason; they killed my brother and a few other warriors who were hunting food for our village. We now have our food back for our people, along with some other things but my brother will no longer walk Mother Earth."

"Spotted Horse, I think our questions have all been answered and that we should now go our separate ways and finish what we need to do."

Bert turned and started to walk away from them, but Spotted Horse had something else to say.

"It is good to see that there is a white man called Buck who is a good person. When we return to our village I will tell our people about you because I like the person who you are."

When the natives rode away, Dan and Kathy rode their horses over to Bert. He explained to them what had happened and that everything was all right now. Dan said that it was good to hear that the ones responsible for his friend's death had also paid the price for it.

Together they rode off toward Sand Stone Creek and after a few days they could see the town in the distance.

As they were riding through the town Bert could tell that the people were acting very curious. So he figured that it was time to stop riding and begin talking.

"Can anyone tell me how to find William Thompson's place because I have a gift for him?"

The sheriff came over to them with two of his deputies and they had their guns pointed at Bert and Dan.

Then the sheriff said, "The two of you get down off your horses, because you're going to jail. I think that the two of you are up to something not right. Who is that little girl?

Kathy spoke, "You are the one doing something not right. Bert and Dan are bringing me to my grandfather's farm, Bert has kept me safe and promised to help me join my family."

Bert then said, "I understand your reactions because I'm sure that Kathy's family has been looking for her since the accident, and that they are worried about her. It is important for me to see her return to her family's arms."

The sheriff put his gun away and told his deputies to do the same.

Then he said, "I apologize for my action to you. You were right about Kathy's family looking for her. They have shown me a picture of her, so when I saw her I only wanted to also bring her home. I would like to escort the three of you to her grandfather's farm because I to would like to see them reunited."

As they rode together to the farm, Kathy told the sheriff all about everything that had happened after the accident. The sheriff thanked Bert for everything and told him that Kathy's mother, father, and grandparents would also be thankful.

When they arrived at the Thompson's farm, Bert was amazed to see such a large place. There were four large barns with separate fenced in areas that had cattle and horses in them. There were also three farmhouses; one was newly built which belonged to Kathy's mom and dad. Her grandparent's home was a much larger home, and a lot older looking. The third home was the place where all the workers on the farm stayed.

When Bert saw Kathy being hugged by her mother, father, and grandparents, he figured that he had accomplished what needed to be done and it was time to go. Kathy and Dan were telling everyone there how Bert had helped her and protected her from any harm. When Dan explained what had happened, when he and his friend first made contact with Bert, the sheriff was surprised that Bert wasn't shot.

As Bert was headed toward the main gate of the farm he went by a fenced in corral area. There was a man trying to ride on the back of a wild horse. The horse was black and tan in color and very muscular looking. The horse tossed a rider off his back onto the ground. He continued running around fast and hard inside the corral. The man stood up on his feet and yelled at some other men who were standing on the fence. He told them to lasso the horse and stop him from moving around. When the horse was secure and his movements were stopped, the rider went over to him and started beating on him aggressively with a leather strap.

Bert yelled at the rider to stop, but he didn't. So Bert went over to the fence and went into the corral and stood next to the rider and told him to stop hitting the horse.

The rider then said, "What are you telling me to stop for? I am the one in charge here and this horse is going to be shown that he has to also do what I want him to do, or he will pay a price. None of my men have been able to train or ride this horse because he is a wild one."

"Yes, he is a wild one and what you are doing to him is only going to make him resist you even more. I can show you how to ride him, but you are going to have to let me do it my way and not yours."

"All right. We will watch you, and we will be laughing when he puts you on the ground and jumps on your back. We will let him beat you and maybe kill you, we will not stop him because you have stopped us."

All the men walked back over to the fence and sat down on the top rail to watch Bert.

Bert untied the ropes that held the horse from doing any movements first. He then removed the saddle off the horse's back and started to pet his neck. Bert looked deep into his eyes and spoke to him quietly.

"I understand that you don't like these men because of how you have been treated by them. The freedom that you once had has been changed to a fenced in area and it is hard for you to accept. I want to help make your experience here at this place better for you. I will give you my respect and I hope that you will do the same for me. And if these men see this, maybe they will learn something important from us."

Bert could tell that the horse was very calm so he felt that it was time for him to try and get on his back. The men on the fence and also the Thompson family couldn't believe the horse didn't react when Bert mounted him. He stood completely still for a while and then he started walking around, he then turned and faced the men who were sitting on the fence rail, he ran fast over toward them. The men jumped down off the rail to the backside of the fence. When the horse came to the fence where the men were sitting he jumped over the fence and stopped because he was now on the same side as them. Bert got down off the horse and stood next to him and spoke.

"When you give respect you are sometimes given it back in return. This horse was born free and wild and you have been trying to take him from his true spirit. He is not use to having a saddle on his back or a person beating on him. If you were him, how do you think you would react to being treated, like you have treated him?"

William Thompson then said, "Bert, you are a very good and a smart man. What you have done for my family and now this animal is a wonderful thing. I would like for you to stay here and work for me because I know that you will do things helpful and correctly. And we could use a man like you here, and that horse is yours my friend. My family and I thank you for keeping Kathy safe and we all hope that you will accept my offer of work.

# CHAPTER FOUR

Morning Star walked over to the mountain lion, wolf, and eagle and thanked them for helping her to unite with her loved ones. She then laid down on the ground and closed her eyes and fell asleep next to them. As she was dreaming her father came to her again and began talking to her.

"Morning Star, I have come to you to help you to understand your destiny. Your fate in the future is of great importance to mankind. You will have another individual at your side and your combined strength will have a great meaning for life on Mother Earth. The two of you will help all the different races of life and their culture to follow the correct path. There will be many challenges for the both of you to face, and I will be there for you both like I am now. Things will be learned by others from the two of you because your souls are true goodness. They will do things the right way because you will help them to see it."

The soldiers saw Bert working on the wagon wheel and rode their horses over to him. They asked him where the Thompson farm was located at and if he knew of a man called Bert. When Bert told them that his name was Bert, they explained to him what had happened at the Indian reservation, and also to their soldiers. Bert felt that he had to go with them so he got up and mounted his horse. He and the soldiers rode off to the area where the soldiers had battled the natives. While they were traveling, Bert and the officer in charge whose name was Joe, talked to each other and became friends.

Morning Star and her animal loved ones were standing together on the mountaintop ridge. The wolf and mountain lion began moving because the eagle took off into flight. They were all watching the direction that the eagle was flying in. Morning Star could see in the far distance a group of horses with riders. As they got closer she could tell that they were soldiers, but one of them was not. He was at the front of the group of soldiers and the eagle was in the sky circling above him. Morning Star knew that she needed to stay focused on him because the eagle was giving her a sign to do that.

Joe was telling Bert that the battle area was on the other side of the mountain stream. Bert was listening to him, but he had a feeling that he and the soldiers were being watched. He kept looking at the mountain for any sign of someone because he felt that there was definitely someone there. The closer they got to the mountain the stronger his feeling got. So he told Joe that he needed to check out the mountain for any sign of anyone being there. Joe said that he and his men would continue to follow the stream for a while longer, and that they would wait for him to return down stream.

Bert crossed the mountain stream and found a safe place for his horse in a ravine on the mountainside. He did not tie his horse's bridle to anything so that he could remain free and safe. He touched his horses face and told him to be careful and alert of any danger. He then started walking in the mountain forest looking for any signs of any human life. There were deer, bear, raccoon, marten, mountain lion, wolf, fox, squirrel, rabbit, and other animal footprints in the forest. As he continued walking up the mountain he then found a footprint of a human being. He also found tracks of a mountain lion walking near the person, so he continued to follow the tracks.

The farther he went, he could tell that it looked like they were going up the mountain together. After a little ways he then heard the sound of guns being fired. He knew that they were the soldiers because the shooting was coming from there direction. So he started running down the mountain toward the shooting of guns.

Morning Star was watching her people attack the soldiers by the stream. She was amazed to see her people shooting guns at the soldiers. The soldiers were returning the gunfire, but some of them had been already wounded and killed because of the surprise attack. She wanted the fighting to stop because she did not like seeing people hurt and killed by each other. As she was wishing and asking for some help to stop the fighting, she saw the man who she was drawn to watch, running on foot toward the fighting.

Bert could see the natives along the edge of the forest shooting guns and also arrows at the soldiers. He felt that he needed to go to them and try to stop what was happening. So he started to run right toward them and as he was he heard a voice tell him that he would be protected because of what he was about to do. A couple of warriors saw him running toward them so they aimed their weapons at him. One fired a gun at him and the other one shot an arrow from his bow, neither warrior hit Bert and they were about to shoot again.

Bert started yelling at them to stop the fighting because if they continued there would be more consequences for them to face. Another warrior now stepped out of the forest and was about to attack Bert, and Bert was ready to respond to his actions. The warrior now realized who Bert was and he began to speak instead of fight.

"I know you. Your name is Buck, and I am one of Spotted Horse's warriors. Are you here to help us fight these soldiers or are you going to fight us?"

"No. I am not here to fight you or the soldiers, but I am here to stop the fighting between you both. I know that there is something not right happening, and if it is not corrected then the fighting will continue and not end now. Is Spotted Horse here because I would like to see him and also talk with him?"

The warrior told another warrior to go and find Spotted Horse. "Tell him to come here quickly, that Buck is here and he needs to speak to him."

After a short period of time Spotted Horse came running over to Buck and asked him a question.

"Are you here to help us win this fight against these soldiers, because we could use you?"

"Spotted Horse, I have all ready answered that question to your warrior standing by me, but I will answer it again for you.

I am here for a reason and it is to try and stop what is happening before it gets worse. I will not ever fight in a battle that I think and feel is wrong, but I will fight to make it stop, when it helps to save lives. Why did you attack these soldiers?"

"Our chief, at our village, has sent me here with our warriors to stop these soldiers from destroying our village."

"Spotted Horse, please believe me and trust what I say because it is the truth. But first we both have to stop the fighting that is going on."

Buck yelled out to Joe and asked him to please stop his men from shooting their weapons so that the fighting could cease. Spotted Horse also yelled to his warriors to stop the fighting now.

The fighting did stop on both sides, and then Bert saw two warriors mount horses. He asked Spotted Horse to stop them from riding away. Spotted Horse ordered the two warriors to get off the horses, but what they did instead was ride their horses toward Bert and Spotted Horse. The two warriors now held weapons in their hands as they approached.

Bert now knew and felt that they were the ones responsible for everything that had happened. He also knew what he needed to do to stop them. He reached down on the ground and picked up two big stones. He threw one stone at one of the warriors, and it knocked him right off his horse. The other warrior stopped his horse and aimed his bow and arrow at Buck and shot the arrow at him. Buck then threw the other stone at the arrow in flight and it hit it and it fell onto the ground broken. Some of Spotted Horse's warriors grabbed the warrior's leg and pulled him down off his horse. Spotted Horse told his warrior's to keep the two of them under guard.

Buck told Spotted Horse about what had happened at

the Berry Indian reservation, and also what had happen to Joe's soldiers, while they were trying to capture them. Spotted Horse told Buck that the two warriors had told their village chief that there was a group of soldiers coming to destroy their village. And that the two of them were survivors from a village that had all ready been destroyed by the same soldiers. And it was why they attacked the soldiers, because they thought that they were coming to their village to destroy it too.

Spotted Horse was now worried that the soldiers would return with others and actually do that. Buck told Spotted Horse that because of what the two renegade warriors had done to both people, they would have to pay the price for both sides. He told Spotted Horse to keep a close watch over the two renegade warriors because they were very distrustful. That he would go over to the soldiers and explain to them why they were attacked, and that the ones responsible for causing it, would be turned over to them. That he would also set up a meeting so that both sides would have a better understanding of each others reason for what took place.

Bert walked slowly over to the soldiers so that they would not feel that they would have to be doing any more fighting. When Bert joined up with Joe he told him that he was sorry that he lost more of his men. Bert explained to Joe what had caused all the problems and that he had the two renegades that had been responsible for it all. Bert told Joe that he felt that it would be good for both sides to show each other respect, honor, and also their sorrow for making a mistake. Joe agreed to going back over with a couple of his soldiers and speaking with Spotted Horse. He then thanked Bert for stopping the fighting that occurred, because if he hadn't there would have been a lot more death done.

•  •  •

Morning Star saw Bert stop the fighting, and she also saw him stop the warriors on horses with stones. The more she thought about his actions, the stronger the feeling of being drawn to him became. When she saw him walk back to the soldiers she felt that she needed to go down the mountain to her people to see if she could help any of the wounded.

Spotted Horse saw Morning Star walking toward them, so he went to her. Morning Star told Spotted Horse that she could help the wounded if he aloud her to. Spotted Horse thanked her for coming to them and giving them her help.

Bert and Joe, along with four other soldiers started walking back over to Spotted Horse and his warriors. Bert had everyone follow him from behind so that they would feel safe.

As they got closer to where Spotted Horse and his warriors were, Bert began calling out to Spotted Horse, "I have returned and the ones with me have come peacefully. They look forward to talking with you. We will stand here until you say it is all right for us to come to you."

Spotted Horse and some of his warriors came over to Bert; they all sat down together and talked to each other for a while. Both sides understood and agreed that what had happened was a mistake because of two liars. Joe told Spotted Horse that he would make sure that the two warriors who were responsible for all the deaths and lies done, would pay a price for all the wrong that they committed.

Morning Star was glad to see her people and the soldiers communicating well together. When Bert looked over at Morning Star he could not take his eyes off of her. He felt that her energy was the same energy feeling, which he had felt, when he was approaching the mountain on his horse. Morning Star could not take her eyes off of Bert either, because she also felt Bert's energy too, and she knew it was good. They both felt that they needed to speak to each other.

Bert then got another feeling so he turned his eyes and looked at Spotted Horse's warriors bringing the two renegades captives to Joe. As they were walking near Morning Star one of them grabbed her from behind and held a knife on her throat. The other renegade warrior now had a knife at his throat. Spotted Horse's warriors kept him in custody. Everyone wanted to attack the one that held Morning Star, but they couldn't because of what the one warrior was doing with his knife.

Bert stood up and said to him, "You have already done too many things wrong. If you want you can take me instead of her, because I'm the one who has placed you where you are now."

"No I am going to leave here with her and when I'm far enough away, I'll let her go."

He started walking backwards with Morning Star, trying to get away from everyone. A wolf began to howl loudly behind him, so he stopped and turned his head to see if the wolf was there. He couldn't see him. The warrior began to move again, the wolf now howled even louder. The warrior stopped moving and turned his head to look once more. Bert moved with great speed and no noise. He stood with his body next to Morning Star.

The renegade warrior didn't even know that Bert was there next to him yet. When he turned his head to look back at the others, Bert grabbed the wrist that held the knife on Morning Star's throat. Bert had strength that he had never felt before and as he squeezed the warrior's wrist with the strength. The warrior screamed out in great pain and dropped the knife onto the ground because he no longer had any feeling in his hand. Bert continued to squeeze his wrist with a lot of pressure. Bert then told him to release the woman that he was holding with his other arm. When he released her, Bert also let go of his wrist, the warrior dropped to his knees and then laid on the ground because of the pain he was in. Spotted Horse's warriors went over to him and stood around him because they didn't want him to do anything. The warrior wasn't even able to move at all because he was too weak from what had just happened to him.

Everyone was amazed at what they had just seen Bert do. Spotted Horse and Joe were standing next to each other.

Joe said, "I have never seen anyone as fast or as strong as you Bert. How were you able to do that? Have you seen anyone do that before Spotted Horse? I am glad that I wasn't the only witness to what this man has just done, because if I was, who would of believed me?"

Morning Star answered Joe's question by saying, "He was given that special strength and speed from his spirit guardians, along with mine as well. He is a good and wonderful man and I thank you, Bert, for keeping me safe from any harm."

Spotted Horse then said, "I know that Buck is a good man because we have met before. But what I have just seen him do tells me that Morning Star is correct about his guardian spirits. I also thank you Buck and your guardians, for helping the soldiers, and us, stop our fighting. We can now both return to our people and tell them the truth about why this happened and how it ended. I understand now that we and the soldiers have to keep our communication open to each other in order to keep peace between us both."

Joe shook Bert's hand and also thanked him and said that he agreed with Spotted Horse. Joe said that he too would tell his commander and other officials that communication does play a very important part in keeping peace. That he and his soldiers were honored to have been able to speak with a warrior called Spotted Horse.

Spotted Horse had his warriors lift the renegade warrior to his feet, and they dragged him over to Joe and his men. Spotted Horse then told Joe that he too was honored to have talked with a white soldier who would do things correctly. Joe then said that he would take the two renegades and make them see the meaning of the word called justice, because of what they have done. Joe and Spotted Horse said goodbye to each other and they both returned to their men.

# CHAPTER FIVE

Morning Star and Bert stood together because they both wanted to talk to each other alone. Bert told her that he needed to go back to the mountain because he had left his horse there. She said that she would like to go with him to help him find his horse. As they walked back to the ravine where he had left his horse, they continued to talk to each other about their different experiences that they needed to face in life. She told him about her father and also Buffalo Tear.

Bert told her that they were two warriors that were always honored and respected at the village he grew up in. And that he was now honored to have met one of his guardian's daughter. He explained to her that the Warrior of Truth had come to him with words of guidance many times.

Morning Star stopped walking and stood facing Bert. She looked deep into his eyes and he did the same. She now knew why she was drawn to him; it was because he was the one that her father had said would be at her side. Bert was happy inside to because he felt that Morning Star was going to be a very important part of his life.

Morning Star started to tell Bert about the sacred mountain and how important it was to be able to take steps on it. Bert knew that it was a very special place the moment he first saw the mountain because he could feel the energy emanating from it. He also knew that it had helped him to stop the fighting and also save Morning Star from getting hurt.

All of a sudden the mountain lion appeared in front of them. Bert stepped in front of Morning Star, but he felt that everything was okay.

"It's alright, Bert. He will not hurt either of us because he is my friend and totem. I think he is here for us to follow him."

An eagle and a wolf then began to callout from the mountaintop. Morning Star now knew that they were both being called to go to the mountaintop.

"Bert, I'm not sure if you have any idea what we are being asked to do. Will you please go with me to the top of the mountain? When we arrive there you are more than likely going to experience something you may never have before."

"Morning Star, I understand what you are saying to me. The village that I grew up in has shown me, and taught me, all about our spirit guardians, and also how to follow the correct path in life for ones self. I would not be here now and neither would you, if we weren't supposed to be. We have been brought together for a reason. I believe that its purpose is very meaningful now. I am excited and glad because of who you are and who I am.

Morning Star and Bert held hands as they began to walk to the top of the mountain. The sun was setting and the stars and moon were lighting up the sky with brightness when they reached the mountaintop. They sat down together and they both told each other that it was wonderful to feel each other's love.

A large white cloud began to take shape in front of them. Bert and Morning Star could see many faces begin to form inside the cloud. A woman's voice started speaking and it brought tears into Bert's eyes because it had been many years since he had heard her speak.

His mother said, "We are your family, my son. We have come to you to tell you that we are all proud of you. You have followed your true inner soul and that has been a wonderful and good thing for life so far. We are happy to see you with another who is also like you. Being in physical form on Mother Earth and who you both are, means that life will have some great help from you both."

Bert's father then said, "Continue your journey, my son, with your strength and ours." As the cloud began to fade Bert felt sad because of all the years he had not seen his parents. Morning Star hugged Bert in her arms. The sadness left his body and it was replaced with joy. Because now he knew and felt that they did not come to him to make him sad. That they wanted to only show him and tell him that they too were watching over him.

Bert and Morning Star held each other close and they fell asleep in each other's arms. They woke up before the morning sunrise so that they could see the sun come up in the eastern skyline. It was beautiful to watch the sky and clouds become red in color as the sun came up.

Bert talked to Morning Star about the Thompson family and how they became good friends of his. She said that she would like to meet them so they decided to go to their farm. Bert and Morning Star began to walk back down the mountain to the ravine where Bert had left his horse. When they reached the place, where he had left him, the horse was not there. So they continued to walk toward the mountain stream and when they reached it, they walked across it. Morning Star and Bert turned around and faced the mountain when they stepped out of the water. Together they thanked the mountain spirits for helping them, and they hoped to return again someday soon.

As they turned to start walking they both could see two horses coming to them. Bert's horse had another one following him as he was walking straight over to Bert and Morning Star. Bert and Morning Star touched and thanked him for coming to them. They also thanked the other horse with him. They both mounted the horses and rode off and it took them only a few days before they arrived at the Thompson farm.

The Thompson family was happy to see Bert return to them and they were also glad to meet Morning Star. They all sat together for most of the day talking to each other. Morning Star was glad to see that she was accepted there and she enjoyed talking to Kathy. The Thompson's offered to hold a wedding ceremony for them at the farm because they could tell that Bert and Morning Star loved each other. Morning Star and Bert thanked them for there generosity and they told them they were honored by their offer.

Later on in the evening when Bert and Morning Star were alone, Bert told her that he also would like to have a ceremony with her people. He wanted to show them his respect and also the love, that he felt for them to. Morning Star agreed that it would be a wonderful and a good thing to do because they would be showing both type of people, red and white their respect. Together they laughed and held each other close in their arms. They then closed their eyes and fell asleep in each other's arms. As they were sleeping, they were both dreaming the same dream. They were being united as one by their guardians and ancestors. All their loved ones from the past were present when Buffalo Tear preformed the ceremony.

He spoke these words, "The two of you will walk Mother Earth together. Love will be the word that will always be the true part of you both because it is your true souls. Your souls will always be connected as one from this day forward, you may not always be together physically, but your souls will be. You both are also a part of us, as we are also a part of you, which means that we are also connected as one. Our physical journey on Mother Earth is over, but yours is still under way and we are all here for you when you are in need of us. We give you strength, courage, wisdom, and knowledge to face anything opposite good and right. The two of you will help life on Mother Earth to follow the correct path because that is your purpose for being there. We love you, and we are proud of you for continuing what we have left behind."

Bert and Morning Star woke up together and they talked to each other about their dreams. They were happy to know that they both had the same exact one together, which meant that they were as one together now.

The wedding ceremony at the farm was a beautiful procedure. A holy man married Bert and Morning Star, and many people came over to them after it and congratulated them. A very old man that Morning Star felt she knew said he was glad to see them together. He also said that he had heard many good things that they had done and that he wanted to speak to them about it when they had some free time.

Bert and Morning Star could tell that he had something of great importance to say to them. So they told him that they could talk to him after the party. He agreed to meet with them later.

When the day was ending and everyone was leaving, Bert and Morning Star went over to William Thompson, Kathy and her parents, and thanked them for everything they had done. William in return thanked them for what they had done with the soldiers because they had saved people's lives. William also told them that a man named Mike wanted to speak to them and that he was a government official who was interested in everything that they had accomplished. Kathy's mother then said, "He also knows all about how you saved Kathy's life and returned her to us, Bert."

Mike saw them talking together so he walked over to them and asked if he could speak with them now. William told the three of them to follow him to his house and that he was going to take them to a room where they could talk together privately.

Mike first said that he was honored to have known Buffalo Tear, and Morning Stars parents, in the past. And that he was very honored now to meet Morning Star as an adult, and also Bert. He told Bert that he had read reports about some of the happenings he had accomplished. That he had also spoke to the individuals who were there personally at the time. He said that he was glad to see a man doing things correctly for the natives and the white people, so there would be peace amongst them. He also said that he knew that Bert had been raised in a native village. So he realized that Bert understood the ways and beliefs of the natives, and that he also respected them because of his actions. He told Bert and Morning Star that he had come to them to ask the two of them to do something. That it would be very important and also have a very special purpose to help civilization now. And that the natives on Mother Earth would still have a long way to go yet, for them to be able to adapt to the changes, that were needed to be faced.

"I think that the two of you can help them to do that and also help the white people to accept and understand the native culture. I know that you both will try to keep both sides at peace. You will also see that there are other different races with different cultures, which you will need to deal with as well. There are people from France, Spain, Britain, Germany, Ireland, Holland, and other countries. That means that their beliefs and cultures will also be a challenge to face in order for peace to be here."

Mike then told Bert and Morning Star that he was getting near the end of his time here on Mother Earth. And that his quest was now to find someone, or two individuals, to be a replacement for his position. He was a spokesperson for all the different races, and that his job was to try to keep peace amongst them all. Mike told them it would be a difficult job at times, but they had to try and get the governments, and the different races, to see and do things the correct and right way for each other. And that there would also be a lot of different conflicts and opinions to deal with because of peoples ways of thinking, as well. But the most important part of the job, was to let them all hear the words that were needed to be said to keep peace and also for things to be done correctly. Mike said that he felt that the two of them would be able to do that job right for everyone.

Mike asked Morning Star and Bert to go with him in the morning. That they would return to his office so that he could introduce them to the associates in his field of work. Mike told them if they felt that they needed some more time together to discuss this matter, he would wait for them and their decision.

Morning Star and Bert already knew that they needed to leave with him in the morning. They felt that they both were being given a quest now to help all people on Mother Earth. So they told Mike that they would go with him in the morning when he was ready because it was what they were suppose to do.

Mike was glad to see the two of them willing to continue doing what he soon would be leaving behind. He knew that he would have to get some of the other government officials to agree with his decision about his replacements in order for Bert and Morning Star to be able to fulfill his seat. But he figured that when the others were in physical contact with Bert and Morning Star that they too would see and know that they were the ones needed for his replacement.

The three of them were preparing to leave the Thompson farm in the early morning. The Thompson family said goodbye to Bert and Morning Star with hugs and kisses. As Bert was hugging Kathy she told him that she hoped to see him again. Bert told Kathy and her family that they should stay in contact with each other because they were more than just good friends. They agreed with him and said that he would always be a part of their family.

As the three of them rode their horses, Mike told Bert

and Morning Star that they were going to ride their horses to a city that had a large fortress. From there, they would be escorted with some soldiers to another very large city on the east coast, called Boston.

Bert then told Mike that he needed to set his horse and Morning Star's horse free before they enter the city and fortress area. Their two horses were wild ones and he wanted them to remain free from any other humans. Mike said that he understood and that he agreed with Bert's feeling about letting the horses remain free in their wilderness home, instead of the city.

During the rest of the days they spent traveling Mike talked about the many different types of situations that they could face and that they would soon begin when they reached the city of Boston. Bert and Morning Star both told Mike that they knew and understood what he was saying. They both had seen and already experienced the different ways of people's thoughts and ideas toward things. They both explained to Mike how they felt about doing things the correct way and that it was important for them to do that for all life on Mother Earth. Mike told them that he was glad to see and hear the words of a man he had once walked beside, come from within them both, the Warrior of Truth.

After a few days of traveling, the city with the fort could be seen in the distance. Bert and Morning Star dismounted their horses and Bert removed the horse's bridles. He then held his horse's face in his hands and began to talk to him. Bert thanked him for being reliable and respectful to him, and he told his horse that he would always hold him in his heart. Bert released his face and told him that it was time for him to return to the wilderness and be safe and free. Bert's horse turned away and started running and so did Morning Star's, but after a short ways he stopped and looked back at Bert. He rose up unto his back legs and waved to Bert with his front legs in the air. Bert wave back to his horse. Together they said, goodbye.

The three of them spent five days in the city before the soldiers came to escort them to the east. During the five days Mike had convinced Bert and Morning Star to change their physical appearance. Bert's hair was no longer braided and long and Morning Star was wearing white women's clothing. Mike had purchased the new clothing for them both so that they would look more like city people instead of wilderness ones.

When the soldiers arrived they had a wagon for the three of them to travel in. They spent many weeks traveling east before they came to a city called New York. It was a very big city with many people. Mike told Bert and Morning Star that he needed to introduce them to some political officials that he knew there. He told the officials that Bert and Morning Star were going to be a replacement for him, but that he would sit along side them for a while to help them. Everyone there seemed to accept his new replacements. After a couple of days in New York they left for Boston.

When they arrived in Boston, Mike took Bert and Morning Star to a building that he said he owned. He told them that they could live there, but he figured that at some time they would decide they would like to live in a quieter place. Mike took them around in the city so that they could see and learn what the city life was all about there. After a couple of days he then took them to his office to introduce them to his associates.

They all knew that he was looking to find the correct replacement for him and they were a little surprised to see two instead of one. After they talked with Bert and Morning Star they were excited and happy about their two new consultants. Because they were all amazed at how Mike had found a couple who seemed to be very knowledgeable about human ways and doing things the correct way. So they all accepted Bert and Morning Star as Mike's replacement.

Bert and Morning Star now had a new challenge to face in their journey on Mother Earth. As the time pasted they became a part of many new happenings. They did experience a lot of different conflicts between the different races and their different countries. They did the best that they could for each race and they continued to follow their path of righteousness with strength.

They raised their son and daughter with true love so that they would both also give it in return to life. When it was their time to leave the government position, a woman whose name was Kathy Thompson replaced them. And she also had to face many challenges; the ones that were the worse were called wars because they caused destruction and pain to all life.

Wars have always been on Mother Earth and they always will be. The reason for them in the beginning of time was because of beliefs and ways of life, and also living it. But as time moved forward into the future many other factors came into existence for the human race. And if we allow these factors to continue, all of life on Mother Earth will end soon, as well.

**PART 3**

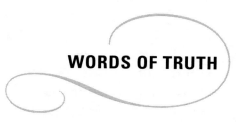

# WORDS OF TRUTH

Beauty is always there, seek it out and it will be seen and felt, heard and smelled.

Listen you will hear.
Look you will see.
Touch you will feel.
Search you will find.
Live you will learn.

Open minds and hearts bring truth, wisdom, knowledge, and love.

Follow your path here on Mother Earth with strength, wisdom, truth, and courage, because it is all needed in order to follow the correct path, here on Mother Earth.

Watch, listen, and learn from the animals here in our world, because they can teach you many things of great importance.

Listen, and you will know; follow, and you will grow. Feel, and you will sense, question and you will understand. Believe and you have what has always been with in you, the truth.

The sun, water, air, and earth, is our energy of life.

While walking on Mother Earth, peace can only be found when you follow your true inner self and soul.

All of life is a part of each other, respect and honor, and you will be.

Beginning and ending, opening and closing, standing and falling, living and dying, are all apart of the cycle in our natural order. These are only rhythms within a larger order that is an endless circle, which means there will be a new beginning.

There has to be a new beginning for us humans because our ways of life now are very wrong. There are many individuals who are wonderful, good of heart and soul. But there are more who are not because they want control, power, and material things, over the one next to them. And in the end if Mother Earth survives our destruction of her, only the pure of heart and soul will have a new beginning. All life will have a new meaning, because what once was will be no more, all will be equal. Love for your true spirit and soul will always be within those who follow it forever. Evil may destroy the human life, but it cannot even touch the spirit and soul of those of pure goodness. That which our Creator gave to us in the very beginning will be there with us always and forever. For those who are lost and blind to it, they need to open up and rediscover the true truth of life here on Mother Earth now.

With each day we are faced with a challenge because it is what life is. Our purpose is to face that challenge with strength and courage and do what is truly right. If one does wrong instead of right, then the path of evil has taken control over you. When that happens, the innocent ones are the ones who suffer the pain. And the ones controlled by the evil, feel no remorse for them, and they continue to follow the wrong path.

We as a human race have made great advancements in our technology, and we have discovered many ways of bettering life. But in going forward we have lost the importance of understanding respect and honor, for each other, and Mother Earth. Power and control is why we have become blind and this will be our demise in the end, if it is not corrected.

When you are looking for answers to your questions, it's not what you bring with, it's what you leave with that matters, and makes the difference.

When it is time to leave the present. What one has touched and said with a pure heart. Will always remain in plain view for those left behind with open hearts and souls.

Your destiny is to be what it is, your journey may take different paths along its way, but the end will be what it is to be, your destiny's purpose.

One must learn to go deep into ones self in order to become open and aware of the true truth that is always there, and present for you. When one's heart is in hand, it is a sign to others to follow their true self's with love.

All of life on Mother Earth is connected, and when one becomes totally extinct so does a part of you.

With each moment something is learned, a teacher is one who can help guide that learning, as long as the teacher is one true of heart and soul.

In all beginnings there is an ending. In all endings there is a new beginning. We are only a part of the circle now, so we must continue to follow it, in order for it to become completely whole for us.

Mother Earth has seen all of life since the beginning; she

can heal, protect, and guide you on your journey to the light. You can receive courage, strength, wisdom, and knowledge from her if one knows how to ask for it from her. Look into the white light and you will know the truth of life. {*Learn*}

When new life is born on Mother Earth it is important that the existing life shows and gives true love. This will teach the newborn life how to give love in return. By also showing the newborn respect, honor, and the meaning of truth, will help the newborn to return it to present life. It is important that we also teach our newborn what our Creator has given us on Mother Earth; our sun, moon, stars, air, water, animals, plants, and mountains. Our Creator and his gifts will help the newborns journey on Mother Earth to be strong and right as long as the newborn remains true to its self and our Creator. Faith in our Creator will protect life and its true meaning. We receive strength and courage to face all challenges of wrong and evil in life from our Creator. When we do things right and follow our correct path we are showing our love and respect for our Creator and life on Mother Earth.

The Mountain Lion totem gives you the power of protection. He teaches you to take charge of your life and make the right decisions when they are needed to be made. He gives you the strength to face the struggling events that can cause you pain and suffering in your life.

The Eagle totem gives you the ability to see things clearly. He gives you the strength to go in the correct direction when faced with a challenge. And he also gives you the ability to turn away from negative and incorrect ways. {White Eagle}

The Wolf totem helps direct you to your true inner self. He gives you the strength of love, courage, and extremely sensitive feelings. You receive the ability of being aware of danger around you. He also gives you the speed to battle against it. {White Wolf}

The Buffalo totem gives you strength to follow the right path in your life. Because of his massive size he can clear your path easily for you as you follow him. He gives you honesty and respect so that you can give it in return. {White Buffalo}

The Bear totem gives you the strength to look inward into your true self. He also helps with healing yourself and others. You receive the ability to face fear with strength and courage from him.

Today, we all know our past and we have come forward to this day in time. Yes, we have evolved and advanced our technology and education. This has opened new doorways for the human race to face on Mother Earth. But now in this day and age we have become more blinded to the true meaning of the word truth than what we were in the past. Respect for life on Mother Earth seems to be losing its true meaning. Many humans can no longer follow or see their true inner soul, even though it is still within them. They allow the words money, control, and power to dominate their lives and their ways of living it. These three words represent the true reason why things are done wrong in our present day an age. Different countries, governments, organizations, religions, and individuals have allowed this wrong to rule over them and control them. And that in return has given life here on Mother Earth only this, destruction of life.

Humans have over populated Mother Earth. We have polluted her earth, her air, her water, and all other life here. Some of the human race has caused their physical strength and bodies to go down hill because of the use of drugs, smoking, alcohol, negative thinking, diet, and not enough exercise. All this has to stop in order for you to be able to work your way to the top of the mountain physically. If you don't change your downward travel in life then you will be the one responsible for your own ending and that is wrong.

The son of our Creator, and also others, has tried to teach and show life here how to follow their correct path. There are individuals out there who are true to themselves and also to others. But there are not enough of them yet to correct the direction of travel, that life is headed in. Because of our actions being wrong and also our thinking, we first see and feel the loss of life. And Mother Earth is also coming to her end sooner then she is supposed too, because of what we have done to her.

Yes, all beginnings have and ending, and all endings may and may not have a new beginning. The may not, is because if they were pure evil inside and it was delivered to life on Mother Earth, their ending should be for eternity.

Some human lives may continue to live in a different part of the universe that is if we are given that option before Mother Earth's ending.

Other life does exist in other parts of the universe and they are much more advanced in every way. Their life's energy is much more pure and stronger than ours because if it wasn't, they would of taken Mother Earth for themselves a long time ago.

Reality now is this, in order for life here to exist. Everyone needs to enter their true soul in order for them to see the real truth. The wrong that is being done now, has got to slow down. It would be even better to totally stop it, but that will not happen at the present time, because it has gotten to strong.

There will be more wars and greater numbers of innocent lives lost. And there will also be more damage done to life from Mother Earth. Severe weather changes will cause devastating storms, tornadoes, hurricanes, snow, earthquakes, volcanoes eruptions, and temper changes. This will happen in our interior atmosphere, and our exterior atmosphere will be this. Our solar system, sun, comets, meteors, planets, stars, and moon, could also cause severe problems that will affect life here on Mother Earth as well.

Mother Earth's rotation has all ready changed and that is one reason way our weather is different now. When our suns energy begins to fade or get stronger, we will even be more challenged for life here on Mother Earth.

There will be a time when our ways of living life here on Mother Earth must change or total destruction will end us all, and that will be our price to pay for all the wrong that has been committed here.

When you let the emotions of hatred, revenge, anger, guilt, depression, fear, and other negative feeling take control over you, you will be taking the wrong steps in life. And this means that you lose the true meaning of the word, Love, because of what you're feeling, and what you're thinking, is not right.

When an individual who is true to themselves has to face another, whom is the opposite of them, conflict could emerge. You need to defend your physical self and inner self with the strength of your true soul, so that you remain the true being that you are.

You are the one who can stop the negative and wrong energy source from taking over your life. It would also be good to help others see and correct it from taking over their lives too. It is your choice and when you are unsure of your decisions, you need to look deeper into your true soul for the correct answers.

You do have guardian angels, spirit guides, archangels, ancestors, and our Creator at your side. When you are in need of them for help you must know how to receive it, and be thankful and respectful to them. The best way to do that is to show our Creator that our actions will be what are also his. True Love, True Respect, True Honesty, True Righteousness, True Truth, is suppose to be the correct way of life on Mother Earth. Stay strong, good, right, and courageous, when faced with the challenges from the opposite side.

There will be changes in our ways of living life today on Mother Earth. These changes have to be soon and they have to be right. Because the direction that life is headed now, is not good for any life. Open your hearts and soul to your true inner self's so that our direction of life will head up the mountain in the correct way, which gives us our only chance for survival of the human race.

While walking on Mother Earth peace can only be found when you follow your true inner self.

On the day of your birth on Mother Earth you have been given a quest. There is a purpose and a reason for you to be here. You are to learn and also to teach. You will have to make the decision to choose the correct path in your life. Some of your steps could be mistakes, but the important thing is that you make them change to be right. Doing this will make your heart and soul pure goodness. And that in turn can affect all life on Mother Earth. We have the Sun, the Moon, the Wind and Air, the Rain and Water, and Earth, to cleanse our bodies and souls to help us to remain strong during our journey. They are a gift to us from our Creator to keep us going. The love that our Creator has given us should be the same love that we give to each other in order for our world to exist.

When ones heart has been touched with Love. It's very wonderful to see and feel.

When you follow your journey's path with righteousness and goodness it helps other life on Mother Earth to also do the same.

# CONCLUSION

This story is only one of many from the past. But it still exists today and at this very moment. You would think that because of our growth in learning and becoming more advanced in all things. That life would be much better here on Mother Earth now, then what it was back in the earlier days. But here at this present time, the human race has become stronger on the bad side, instead of the good. There are many reasons for this and they use to be separate on the list, but now they are at the number one spot. Control, power, and money over the one standing next to you, is what it's all about now. In the past money or gold wasn't as strong as it is today. Money is the cause of every situation in the world today because we have allowed it to control our lives. Do you think that you could survive without it? You may think you can, but the individual at your side cannot. We have over populated Mother Earth now, and because of that, our problems have become much larger. All the different beliefs in religion, governments, and life styles, have caused great conflict amongst all human races.

The evil and wrong doing is over powering that which is good and right. We are destroying ourselves and also Mother Earth. And if things do not change very soon this world will be no more, because of us. Mother Earth is so polluted now, we may not even be able to correct it in time. Earth, air, and water, if we lose only one of the three elements completely, then we are also done here. The wars that we have now are so much more destructive, then in the past. The reason is technology and no communication or understanding for life, and this has taken way to many innocent lives. When one says he kills for his god, he will some day face his god, and then true justice will be served. Everyday I can see the weakness in the human race, which is controlled by evil. Children and elders being mistreated and hurt by individuals who have lost themselves to evil. Greed and material items also play a major roll in our time. I know that there are some who walk Mother Earth who know and understand that all life has a connection. They know how to follow the correct path in life, and they try to help others to see and also follow their true inner self's of goodness. We are all equal and should be treated that way, but we are not treated equal because respect has been lost. The problems now, are the same as the ones from the past. But now they are much more controlling over us, because most of us have closed our minds and inner souls to the truth. The truth is right in front of us, just like it always has been. But many people seem not to want to follow it, or believe it, because of what one might lose. That means that your strength of goodness has become weak. There has to be a new beginning for us humans because our ways of life right now are wrong. There are many who are wonderful and good of heart and soul. But there are more who are not, and that's because they want that control, power, and material things over you. In the end, if Mother Earth does survive all of our destruction of her. Then only the pure of heart and soul survivors, will have a new start on Mother Earth. All will be equal then, and love will be the only true fact for us. Respect, love, and truth will be the new beginning, and those who do have it now, know that it will continue to be forever. Evil may have the power to destroy everything, but it cannot even touch the spirit and soul of those who knows that evil is, what it truly is. All that our Creator gave to us in the very beginning will always be with us. And for those who have lost their sight of it, they need to look deeper within themselves to rediscover it, because the truth is there.

# MOUNTAIN SPIRIT: AUTHORS NOTE

In life there is two of everything, good and bad, sadness as well as joy, losing and winning, falling down and standing up, not enough, as well as too much. Life is a journey sometimes walked in light and sometimes in darkness. You did not ask to be born but you are here. You have weakness as well as strengths within you. Within you, you have the strength to face life and also the fear to turn away from it. You can gain strength from your inner self to face life and all its happenings. You must stand strong in the storms that life can create and face all that is bad with goodness. Being strong means taking one more step to the top of the mountain. No matter how weak you may be, you must keep looking for the correct answer to your questions. Each step you take, you learn what it is that you need to keep you going in the correct direction. You must continue because the closer you get to the top the stronger you become. A new sun rises and a new beginning of a new day is waiting for you. No matter how difficult the step becomes you must continue your journey because it is your destiny.

# MOUNTAIN SPIRIT: ACKNOWLEDGMENTS

A *special thank you* Everyone I have communicated with at Tate Publishing has been wonderful. I am proud of them all for showing their respect and honesty to me, and also to others. I am also proud that they have become a part of my journey on Mother Earth. Thank you all for bringing my project to reality. I also thank Sherry, Wayne, Shelly, and Penelope for their statements, encouragements, proofreading, and knowledge, in helping me to bring my project into your hands. It has been a project of mine for many years. I also thank you for holding and reading *Warrior of Truth*.